MOVILLE LIGHT

*To Ruth
hoping that these stories
meet with your
approval
Best wishes
Judith*

Judith MacCafferty

First published in Great Britain in 2011
by Running Water Publications, London

Typeset by Running Water Publications
Printed and bound by BookPrintingUK, Peterborough

Judith MacCafferty has asserted
her right under the Copyright, Designs and Patents Act, 1988,
to be identified as author of this work.
© Judith MacCafferty, 2011

This book is sold subject to the condition that it shall not,
by way of trade or otherwise, be lent, resold, hired out or
otherwise circulated without the publisher's prior consent
in any form of binding or cover other than that
in which it is published and without a similar
condition including this condition being imposed
on the subsequent purchaser

All characters appearing in this work are fictitious.
Any resemblance to real persons, living or dead, is purely coincidental.

Cover design by Andrew Wanliss-Orlebar

ISBN 9780954471835

for
Veronie
& Des

Contents

Moville Light 7
The Ladder 15
Eternal Fish 25
Watching 31
Close Your Eyes Little Sister 40
Alice's Pipistrelles 49
The Two O'Clock Train 64
The Horizontal Method 71
Bad Dreams 78
Half and Half 87

Moville Light

Liam Skelly was asking his brother for money. He didn't mention that Celia had put him up to it.

'Only a loan. I'll be going away, I promise you.'

'I wouldn't give you a ha'penny. The only place it would go would be down your gullet.'

'You'd be well rid of me.'

'I'll never get rid of you, Liam. A disgrace to the family is what you are.'

Liam said nothing. He wanted to swing for Barney but his brother was bigger than him and there'd be no point in coming away with a bloody nose. That was one thing he'd learned in all his thirty years as Barney's younger brother. He looked round the kitchen, still the same as it had been in his mother's time. Josie hadn't changed it, thank God, a dark tiled floor, the dresser with its blue and white delph. The view over the lough his mother loved to gaze on when she was washing the dishes. Barney always said that Liam was her favourite.

'I want the money now,' Liam dared himself to say, 'you owe it to me.'

'Owe it to you? I owe you nothin'. Nothin' at all.' Barney's voice rang off the walls. Liam took a step backwards. Water off a duck's back, he told himself.

'I want you outy our house. D'you think me and Josie want our weans seeing you staggering home every night?'

Liam left.

At eight o'clock that night he staggered into Peggie's, his third pub of the day. It was a dark brown bar with wooden benches and tables and a tobacco ceiling. He sat down on the back bench, out of sight of the door. He was glad the pub was quiet – he didn't want to speak to anybody. He drank two pints of Guinness and two whiskey chasers. After that he was rightly. His head swam. He knew he should have something to eat but he didn't want to waste the money. He ran a tab in Peggie's that Barney didn't know about, but it would have to come out some time. He hoped he would be far far away by then. Him and Celia. She had plans for them both. She said they should go away to England, get jobs there. It wouldn't be difficult, she said, thousands of other people did it. Liam wasn't so sure.

'It's all right for you,' he'd said, watching the sunlight on her fair hair, 'but what could I do?'

'Isn't London coming down wi' bars? You could get a job in any one of them.'

Celia took his breath away. She was always so enthusiastic about everything. He didn't deserve her. He often felt like the broken hulk lying off the rocks at Carryknock, a sodden mess of wrecked timbers. What did she see in him? He couldn't even guess. Now he wanted her here beside him, but she'd be away to her bed at this time of the night.

He moved to a seat near the fire before he ordered another pint. He would make this one last longer. The fire was dying back, the peat lengths like miniature red logs. He wished that Micky, the skinny barman with the bald patch, would come over and stoke it up, he didn't dare do it himself. He wanted to be good and warm before throwing out time so that when he walked down along the shore, he wouldn't be freezing. He couldn't go home tonight, that was for sure. What did Barney and Josie think when he didn't come home, did they even notice? All Barney seemed to care about was money and making more of it. Their father had divided everything between them when he died, but Barney paid no heed to that. If and when Liam left, Barney would be well chuffed.

At last Micky shouted time and Liam pretended to drink the last dregs from his glass but there was nothing there to drain. He'd spoken to the man next to him, Jimity Paddy, an old soak who spent every night in Peggie's. Paddy had fought in the Battle of Jutland in 1916 and he never tired of telling you about it. He, Liam, wasn't an old soak, it was just a temporary thing, he would be better in a while, things would change, yeah, things would definitely change.

He slunk out of the pub. He didn't want anybody to follow him or realise that he wasn't going home. By tomorrow Barney might have calmed down. He crossed the street. The lights were still on over the Bay Cinema so he knew the film hadn't finished yet. There would be the half ten bus to Greencastle but he wouldn't be on it. He walked down the unlit lane beside the Foyle Hotel, his footsteps echoing in the darkness. The Green stretched to right and left of him. The sea lay below, where the pale light of the moon made a path that nobody could ever walk on. He turned left, away from the town.

The wind whistled in his ears and round his ankles. A nice enough night to be abroad, he told himself, at least it wasn't raining. He had a pee in the public convenience and continued downhill, to where the shore path led along the rocks with the sea glimmering and shoughing a few feet away. It was comforting, for a wee while, but you could get sick of listening to it when you knew it would never stop.

He'd thought there'd be nobody on the Green at this time of night but he was wrong. In the first beach shelter he could make out the shuddering shapes of courting couples and see the red dots of cigarettes. For a moment he tried to imagine himself and Celia entwined in a place like that, but it was far too public. The double seats in the back row of the Bay Cinema were their favourite. That shelter was too close to the town anyway so he moved on. This part of the Green made him think of summer Sundays when his mother would bring them to mass in Moville. Afterwards, she'd buy them ice cream at the Cosy Nook Café and they'd eat it as they strolled down the path. He could feel the chill of the ice cream melting off the cone down his fingers, and his mother wiping his chin with a hankie that smelt of lavender.

The path wound round a bluff and the lights of the town disappeared from view. Out in the bay he could make out the giant malevolent spider of Moville Light as it flashed. When he got to the bathing boxes there were people in there too. He couldn't see them in the dark and they couldn't see him, good job too, but he could hear them. Why was everybody in the world having a good time except him?

The booze was crystallising in his veins. He'd had enough of all this, of things never working out in his favour. He thought that each time he got to this part of the path. How many times had he done this? He'd lost count. The beach was flat and dreary. He felt as if he were walking forever down this stretch of shore, walking away from the few people he'd ever loved. Stop feeling so bloody sorry for yourself. Things would turn out all right; he was certain of it. He and Celia would go away, they would have a great life together and to hell with Barney. He sat down on the edge of the cement path and dangled his legs over the shingle. He stayed there for a long time before moving on.

Liam reached the last shelter. That morning he'd borrowed Barney's greatcoat from the hook in the hall, he'd be busy behind the bar all night, he wouldn't be needing it. He pulled the muffler from round his neck and rolled it into a pillow. He spread himself out on the stone bench that ran round the inside of the shelter. If he curled up in the angle the wind wouldn't get to him, or it would get to him less. It was like rolling up into a ball, uncomfortable for anybody except a hedgehog. He draped the coat over his legs and feet and composed himself for sleep. That's what he called it, composing himself. He could hear his mother saying a prayer when he was wee, Four corners of my bed, four angels at my head. How he missed her! What would she think of him now? God alone knows. A surge of shame washed over him.

The waves hissed gently on the beach, over and back, over and back. He knew that if he watched them they would lull him to sleep but he didn't want to fall asleep sitting up. He conjured up a vision of Celia, in her red winter coat, her hair streaming out behind her, to comfort him, to warm him a wee bit. He was afraid to tell her how much he loved her, afraid of the effect it might have. Would she ever forgive him for these lapses? She was an easygoing girl, but not that easygoing. Celia. He held her name in his head till he fell asleep. His body churned fitfully on the stone bench.

Waking to a cold grey dawn was miserable as sin. Liam's head throbbed as loud as a tractor and his mouth was as dry as a bale of summer straw. Through my fault, through my fault, my own bloody fault. He stood up unsteadily, flexed the stiffness of each muscle. He wished he were miles away. Moville Light rose enormous against the sky. He would walk farther along the shore path now, to where it dwindled out. He clambered among rocks slippery with seaweed. It was better than walking along the road to Greencastle. He was glad to get out of the dank smelly shelter.

Bright green swords of montbretia, nearly as tall as he was, covered the fences along the way. He knew the name because his mother had some in her garden. He could see her down on her knees, pulling up weeds as if her life depended on it. There was another name for the plant, but he'd forgotten it. He loved the brilliant flames of the flowers in summer but now in March there were none. When he passed the holly tree at the bottom of Drumaweir, he knew he was well on his way. Nearer to what he still called home, a drink, oh God a drink, and depending what mood Josie was in, something to eat. He skirted muddy puddles, and then he trod in one and the water seeped to his socks. Must get them shoes mended. But he knew he wouldn't, he only had the one pair. It was misery every time it rained.

He was walking up the hill now, through the tawny skeletons of ferns, chest high, they were brushing Barney's coat with their brittle stems. Hidden among them was the odd bramble, what his father had always called nature's barbed wire, catching on the rough tweed cloth. Jesus, I hope Barney doesn't notice, or Josie, more like. She'd know rightly he'd borrowed the coat. His mouth tasted like a rusty tin. What he needed was a hair of the dog, but Barney would have everything firmly under lock and key until opening time.

There was a dense green smell of damp. He crept along the edge of Donnelly's farm. Geese honked in the distance. He was nearly to the back of the house. He opened the gate into the yard. It was clean and tidy – Josie had seen to that – but there was still a faint stench of beer from the row of discarded barrels against the far wall. The smell tortured him, making his tongue enormous in his mouth till he thought he would choke. It was no word of a lie to say that he would kill for a drink. As he skirted the yard, making for the back door, he put his hand in the pocket of the coat. He touched a cold bunch of keys, so cold his hand let go again. Barney's keys, the keys of the bar! He stopped to think. Josie should be in the kitchen, making Barney's breakfast. Barney would be in the bathroom shaving.

He left the yard by the same gate and walked round to the front of the house. He took the keys out and chose one. He moved towards the dark green door of the bar with its stained glass. He looked up and down the road. There was nobody about. He turned the key in the lock. A rush of expectation and longing flooded him, in ten seconds he would be getting a drink and it wouldn't be a drink of water, that was for sure. The bar was dark and shadowy, even with the reflections of the mirrors. The stools were upended on the tables and there was the stink of old tobacco. Under his feet the floor was slippery with beer.

He turned in behind the bar. He reached for a glass from the rack above, a pint glass. He placed it under the beer pump, the nearest one, he didn't care. He was raising his right hand to the brass handle when a great hairy paw came down on top of his. Liam jumped back, his heart thumping in his chest.

'Christ, Liam, what are you at now? Not only a drunkard but

a bloody thief. Here you are wearing my coat, stealing out of my bloody pub! I thought you said you were leaving!'

He wanted to say, It's my pub as well as yours, didn't my father leave it to the both of us, but his tongue was stuck to the roof of his mouth. Two years now, ever since his father died, he'd worked in the bar for peanuts. What was he, Barney's slave?

Ten minutes later, Liam was walking past the farm again. The only drink he'd had was from the old pump in the yard. His head hurt as if a conger eel were twined tightly round it. His mouth was still as dry as chaff, shucked of spittle. He fingered the stubble on his cheek and ran his hand through his hair. A bird's nest it must look like. What would Celia say? Did he want to think about her? He could see her bright face, hear her light cheery voice. He looked over the hedge to the right. Her house was about five hundred yards away. She would still be there, getting ready to go to school, he couldn't even remember what class she was teaching this year. Wee ones, maybe, wee innocent weans. Weren't they the lucky ones, spending the whole day in her company. Should he go over and tell her what had happened? He could have a drink, maybe. All at once he was desperate to see her, to hear her voice, to tell her, oh God, that Barney had turned him down when he asked for the money. What would she say? He didn't care, he just wanted to tell her. He turned into the next field and realised that he couldn't go climbing through the thorny hawthorn hedges. He'd have to go the long way round, by the road. He pulled the collar of the coat up round his ears and made his way up the hill.

It didn't take him long. Five cars passed him going towards Moville, but he didn't even glance at them. He scrambled down the narrow lane. It was only when he knocked at the varnished front door and Celia's mother answered, that he remembered his scarecrow appearance.

'Dear God in heaven, Liam, what's happened to you? What are you doing here at this time of the morning?' She stared at him and for a minute he thought she wasn't even going to let Celia know he was there.

'Celia,' she called, 'there's a bold bucko here to see you. Looks like he's been through a hedge backwards.'

Celia came from the back of the house. Her hair was tied back with a red ribbon, she was neat in a blue skirt and a white blouse. His Celia.

'The state of you!' was all she said. She didn't touch him.

He plunged straight in.

'Barney…'

'What about him?'

'He… he wouldn't give me a halfpenny.'

'Isn't that the great piece of news?'

'I'm sorry…'

'You've been out on the tear.' She clicked her tongue in disgust and turned away.

'Nothing I could do.'

'No point, Liam,' she said. She went back inside and closed the door firmly behind her, without a backward glance.

So that was that.

He pulled the coat around him again, chilled in the cool morning air. It was a wonder to God that Barney hadn't ripped it off his back. He stumbled away from the house, the tears tripping him, down the path that led to the beach. The sea was grey and choppy. There was a boat out in the channel, the Scotch boat, the ferry to Glasgow. As its dark bulk steamed past Moville Light, Liam wished he were on it, going somewhere, anywhere. Celia didn't want him, he couldn't take it in. He knew now that he couldn't leave here, couldn't leave the place where he was born, where his mother had brought him up, where she was buried in Ballybrack churchyard. He knew that if he left, he could never come back, never walk this way again. He shuffled onto the hard sand, his feet leaving scarcely any prints. He would walk on into the sea, he would just walk on, way out past the Light.

The Ladder

I'm sitting here at the window in my usual seat, my eyes out on stalks for a sight of Mick Deeney. He doesn't always go in and out of the front door but sometimes that one does. Just to show she's the boss, not a servant or anything. The big fat eejut.

Understand me now, I don't want to marry Mick Deeney for love. I don't believe in all that oul codology. There's our Hugh, got married to Nettie last week, at his age, it's ridiculous to be behaving like love's young dream. It'll soon wear off, we all know that and then they'll be at each other's throats, once Nettie realises how much Hugh is used to me dancing attendance on him. I'd be willing to do the same for Mick Deeney.

I'm watching him now, coming down his front steps, wearing his old corduroys. He's not exactly handsome, is Mick, and he's as bald as a coot but since his aunt died last year and left him a poke of money, I've got interested in him. I'm a fine looking woman in the prime of life and my pastry making skills are known the length and breadth of the country.

Last week at Hugh's wedding, I went over and spoke to Mick, asked him how he was getting on, how the farm was, how many sheep and cows and hens he had. He was shy at first – all he would say was, 'I've just got the half dozen cows now, quite enough for me to milk, quite enough.'

He may need someone to help him out with the milking but that wasn't what I had in mind. I just want to be Mrs., Mrs. Michael Deeney of Culleybackey Farm. Beats being Miss Lizzy Malley, spinster of this parish. I don't want that on my tombstone, thank you very much.

'I'm a neighbour of yours now, Mick, did you know that?' I said to him. He looked surprised. I had persuaded my darling brother Hugh to buy me this lovely new bungalow right opposite the farm. He thought he could palm me off with some poky wee shoebox of a flat in town but I said to him, 'That house that Jimmy Doyle built for his poor mother would be fine for me,' and in the end he bought it. I knew it would be cosy and comfortable and grand for spying on your man.

'I didn't know that, Lizzy,' Mick says to me. 'Isn't it a bit far out of town for you if you don't drive a car?'

'If I'm ever in a jam,' I sing, 'I'll call on you.'

But Mick didn't get the chance to reply because at that moment Eithne O'Neill, that keeps house for him, came up and says, 'D'ye you think you could run me home now, Mr. Deeney?'

Would you believe it, they asked her to be Hughie's bridesmaid. Nettie has no sisters but they didn't even consider me. Eithne, the biggest backside in Tullydish, was dressed in this fluffy pink outfit that made her look like a giant dollop of candyfloss. I'm surprised the priest let her come up to the altar looking like that. If I was that enormous, I wouldn't want to be showing all that flesh below my double chins. I'm only half the size of her and I was wearing my best charcoal grey suit and my late mother's fox fur and there is not another woman present who looked as smart as me. But Mick was a soft touch particularly where the Eithne O'Neills of this world are concerned. So I didn't manage any more conversation but I couldn't get him out of my head.

I sit here beside the window and worry about her. She's there every day, she's in there now. I have to think about what they could be getting up to behind closed doors. How can she be called Eithne

The Ladder

O'Neill, isn't that a name for a thin person, not a round fat name like Maura Corcoran in the shop who is as skinny as a pane of glass? I've placed my mother's old armchair between the bed and the window, where I've put up my new net curtains, so that I can watch out for Mick without him seeing me. What I hadn't counted on – you don't always realise the drawbacks to things before you do them, I've often noticed that – was that I'd have to watch the comings and goings of Elephant Eithne as well. Shaking her duster out in the mornings, sweeping the steps and sometimes, but not often enough, scrubbing them.

I'm sure she isn't feeding him properly, he looks as if he never ate a good Irish stew in his life, God only knows what rubbish she puts up for him to eat. Isn't she always down in Corcoran's spending his money buying expensive tins and packets, not bothering to cook him a decent meal. Now if I was married to him, I would be in there with a good hot dinner every night and even at lunch time if he came in out of the fields cold and wet, I'd have a big bowl of home made soup on the table, hot and savoury and steamy, none of yon packetty rubbish, and a good fresh wheaten farl to eat with it. That one, the big arse, has no more idea about feeding a man than she has of rising and flying in the air. She's worse than a priest's housekeeper. They never know how to cook, I think God must send them as a punishment to poor parish priests who have to put up with them to the end of their days. I'm thinking of Father Mooney who came round when it all happened. In one way I was lucky it was him and not the gardai – that kept me out of a great deal of trouble.

Now that I don't have Hughie to look after, I have plenty of time for watching over the way, a ringside view of all the comings and goings at Culleybackey Farm. I hate even getting up to go in the kitchen to make a cup of tea – spying on people is thirsty work – so I've bought myself a new electric kettle and put it on a wee table beside the window, with a cup and saucer and the milk and sugar. Now I don't have to desert my post when something interesting is happening. Like the day Elephant Eithne sprained her ankle. I wished she'd broken her leg, I can tell you. You wouldn't credit it, she actually washed the step that morning, a cold icy morning, and of course, the water froze straight away. When she came out at twelve o'clock to go home, she slid right down the steps on her big backside and landed on the gravel path. I was laughing that much, I nearly knocked the boiling kettle over and scalded myself. I didn't move from my post, she screamed and roared out of her like a stuck pig and then Mick came up from the back field. I didn't enjoy that part so much, him helping her up and sitting her down on the steps, he even made her a cup of tea. I wanted to be over there offering him a cup of tea and some of my scones. Hugh used to say that he would kill for half a dozen of my fresh scones with the butter melting into them.

Mick called Dr. Shields and he came round and bandaged up her ankle. Then Mick took his car out – his car! that he only takes out on a Sunday when it's raining and he doesn't want to walk to Mass in his best suit – and ran her home. He helped her into the seat and even spread a rug over her knees, before he climbed in beside her and drove away. I could hardly bear to think about it, the two of them sitting next to each other and his hand not an inch from her knee when he changed gear. I just hope she was in too much pain to be enjoying the situation.

When she fell down the steps, I saw my chance. I could be over there every day, just like her, only I would cook him all the lovely meals I have ever imagined for him, and in the end he would see what he was missing and he would ask me to marry him. Amn't I well set up with my bungalow and he doesn't have to worry about money. Wouldn't I do for free what he pays Elephant Eithne for? We'd make a handsome looking couple and Hugh could give me away. I wouldn't have Nettie for a bridesmaid though, she's too much of an oul drip and anyway she never asked me.

The first day I took him over a tureen of thick vegetable soup, made with a ham bone. I says to Mick, I says, 'I know your amanuensis is off sick,' (I liked that word, I pronounced every syllable, I didn't want him thinking I only went to the primary school like your woman), 'would you like some of this, I've made enough for two?'

Mick looked at me. I hardly knew where to put myself with those two hard blue eyes staring at me, and he says, 'Thank you, Lizzy, that's very thoughtful of you but it won't really be necessary, sure I can manage fine for myself.'

I was incensed (is that the word?) I felt like taking him out and trouncing him up and down the yard. I mean who does he think he is, treating me like that? I had already worked out all the menus for a week and a shopping list written down for Corcoran's. But I didn't show how annoyed I was. I didn't come up with the first snowdrop. I said, 'Sure you've got your work cut out for you with the cows and the hens, and all that land, you don't want to be coming in at night with nothing hot to put in your stomach.'

Mick stroked his chin in that slow way he has and said, 'I suppose you might have a point there, Lizzy.' I could see he still wasn't keen on the idea. 'Right,' I said brightly, 'I'll bring your dinner over at six o'clock, if that would be convenient.'

'That would be grand,' Mick said though he still didn't sound convinced. Honestly I could have crowned him. Some people don't know when they're well off.

After a couple of days (Irish stew, a beautiful haddock pie topped with creamed potatoes, so gorgeous it looked like something out of a magazine, rhubarb crumble, apple snow – not really a good choice that one, a man wants something solid and sugary in the line of puddings, not a wee light flyaway thing) Mick says to me, 'You're a right good cook, Lizzy, I'm really enjoying these meals. Eithne, you know, she cooks very plain things.'

I snorted. Plain things! More like tasteless. You couldn't even refer to her as a good plain cook. I could just imagine her, lying at home, funnelling food down her throat like a vacuum cleaner, thick sandwiches of white bread, thick with salad cream, thick as her big white bottom.

'It's no bother,' I said, 'no bother at all.' Maybe I was on to something at last.

'I'm going over to see Eithne,' Mick said in that gormless way

The Ladder

he has, 'I think I'll take her a slice of that cake you brought me for tea yesterday. It was as good as my old Ma's Christmas cake, was that fruitcake. Terrible rich.'

Rich is right. You'd have to be a millionaire to make a cake like that every week with all them currants and sultanas and lemon peel and Demerara sugar in it, it cost me a fortune down at Corcoran's but nothing is too good for Mick. Wasting it on your woman, has the man no sense? I was spitting mad.

But even though I held my tongue, it didn't do me one whit of good. In no time at all, your woman was back at work and me and my wonderful cooking were banished to the other side of the road and I was back where I started, sitting in my mother's armchair, looking out the window. That's when I got really browned off with him. He didn't seem to realise what a treasure he had in me, he couldn't seem to see the difference between me and Fatso O'Neill. Those blue eyes of his must be as blind as a bat. So I decided to try something different.

I knew he would be working in the hay loft, moving the bales down so that he could feed the cattle, so I fixed that ladder for him. When he went to town on Saturday and Elephant Eithne was out of the way, I went over to the barn. I laid the ladder down flat and I took out a hacksaw I'd pinched from Hughie's toolbox. I sawed through the third rung from the top. I'm just as handy with tools as I am with the rolling pin. Then I put a dab of glue on it and stuck it back in place and when I put it against the wall, you couldn't see a thing. I wanted him to fall down and I'd rush over and rescue him and he would be so grateful to me, we'd be hitched in no time at all.

The next morning I was watching out the window as usual and Mick was working in the barn. I heard this terrible roar. I ran across the road to the barn and Mick was lying on the ground and Miss Eithne O'Neill was standing there, screaming out of her.

'What's the matter?' I asked.

'There's been an accident,' she cried, the big dumb cluck.

'Go and phone for help,' I shouted at her, taking her by the arm and pointing her in the direction of the house.

The Ladder

I knelt down and held Mick Deeney's hand as if my very life depended on it. His face was grey and his eyes were closed but he was still breathing.

'You're going to be grand, Mick, you're going to be grand.'

I took his old bald head and laid it in my lap. Thank God I couldn't see any blood, I knew I'd faint at the sight of blood. The poor man was lying there and it was all my fault. I could have banged my head on the stone floor. The ladder was still propped against the beam and the rung was hanging sideways. I'd attend to that in a minute.

After a while I heard a car pull up outside. The doctor, I thought, at last. But Father Mooney came through the door. Father Mooney! That fat eejut had phoned for the priest instead of an ambulance. Father Mooney looked at me and I have to admit, I must have looked a right sight, down on my knees in my second best tweed skirt and my old blue jumper, holding Mick Deeney's head in my arms. The priest got down on his knees and took Mick's pulse.

'He's alive,' I said impatiently, 'we need to get him to the hospital.'

Father Mooney looked at me. This wasn't turning out at all the way I'd planned it.

'The poor man's in a terrible state. What happened?'

'I don't know,' I said, 'I heard this roaring.' He went over and looked at the ladder, pulled it down on the ground and inspected the broken rung. Far too nosy for my liking.

He turned to me and said in a low voice, 'This was done deliberately. Do you know anything about it, Lizzy?'

'Me, father?' I was all innocence. 'Sure what does it matter now, we need the ambulance.'

'I'm not sure if we need the ambulance at all. I think maybe it's too late. Anyway Dr. Shields is on his way up.'

'Holy Mother of God,' I said, 'the man is far from dead. He was breathing a minute ago.' My knees were starting to hurt and the stone floor was as cold as charity.

'Maybe it's the guards we need to call,' Father Mooney said, 'this looks very suspicious.'

He was still looking at me as if I had just crawled out of a bale of hay. I could see that he wasn't fooled for a minute.

'Are you sure you weren't in here with Mick? Youse weren't up to something?'

'Father dear,' I said to him, losing my patience, 'are you out of your mind? A respectable woman like meself?'

'I thought you might have had designs on him. You do realise, don't you, that you might have killed him.'

'Well, I didn't,' I snapped. 'He's still breathing whatever you say. Amn't I sick to death of him, he never pays any attention to me.' I thought of all the carefully cooked meals I had carried over to him and then I wondered how I had got myself into this situation. Our Hugh would laugh his leg off if he heard about it, not to mention the rest of the town.

Father Mooney was still fiddling with the rung of the ladder. He'd put his glasses on so that he could see it better.

'That's not a reason for killing a man. Anyway what were you expecting him to do? Go down on one knee and propose to you? Sure the man's a confirmed bachelor and always will be. Might as well expect me to propose to you,' he reasoned. I had to hand it to him, the man was as sharp as a tack. But I wasn't behind the door either. I'd go to confession as soon as I could and he wouldn't be able to tell anybody.

'I'm sorry, father,' I said as contritely as I knew how, looking down at the floor. 'Will you be calling the guards now?'

I could hear the siren of the ambulance in the distance.

Father Mooney didn't answer me. He pulled the ladder to the far corner of the barn. Dr. Shields came through the door. The priest went to meet him.

I relinquished Mick Deeney into the hands of the doctor. I got off my knees and dusted down my skirt and thought it was about time I was back in my own house, having a good strong cup of sweet tea.

'I'll be talking to you later, Lizzy,' Father Mooney said as I left

The Ladder

the barn. Silly oul eejut. I looked in the kitchen window as I passed the farmhouse but Elephant Eithne was nowhere to be seen. Not much good in a crisis, that one.

I never slept a wink that night. I kept thinking that the guards were going to ring my doorbell, you never know with priests. They're supposed to be bound by the seal of the confessional, but you just never know, do you? But there's no flies on me, Lizzy O'Malley. The very next day, just to make sure, I walked down to the chapel to go to confession. I sat in the darkness of the box, till Father Mooney slid the shutter back like a trap opening.

'Bless me, father, for I have sinned,' I said to him. 'I tried to kill somebody.'

'Did ye now! Kill somebody!' Father Mooney said in such a loud voice that I thought the whole church would hear him.

'You know that's a mortal sin?'

'I do, father.' The man was a pain.

'No other sins?'

No, I told him. What other crimes did he think I'd committed? He gave me five rosaries to say for my penance and I thought that was the end of it.

Of course I went to the hospital to visit Mick and brought grapes (the best money could buy) and later on when he was better, egg custards and trifles (I even put a wee nip of sherry in, he liked that) but things were never the same again. Mick didn't come back to the farm, he went to live with his married sister, and a young couple took over the farm.

He was never right at himself afterwards. I missed him. I missed talking to him when I went over for my eggs and I missed sitting at the window, watching the farmhouse. I missed coming back in the car with him from Mass on wet wintry Sundays.

Two years later he died. I thought about all that lovely money that was going to go to his sister. Father Mooney took the funeral and I cried my eyes out, I had two lace handkerchiefs wet through. Hugh kept turning to look at me but I didn't care. I stood right up at

The Ladder

the edge of the grave in my best black outfit and I was one of the first to throw a handful of earth down. Elephant Eithne was there, wider than ever, but I never even passed the time of day with her. She was wearing a red coat, so unsuitable for a funeral.

As I was leaving the cemetery, Father Mooney came over and whispered, 'I see you've regretted your evil deed, Lizzy.'

'Wasn't he the lovely man, Father,' I said out loud. Under my breath I swore. That smart alecky priest has my heart scalded. He comes over to my house twice a week for his tea. He expects a real slap up meal, the best cooking I can do. He'll probably keep on till he's holding my funeral service. Blackmailed I'll be for the rest of my life, just because I wanted to be Mrs. Michael Deeney.

Eternal Fish

'You know I've never liked fish,' the man cried as he caught hold of the finny creature on the plate. He whirled it round his head like a shot putter swinging the lead. When he let go they were showered with flakes of wet fish. The backbone came to rest in a plant on his left, the spines embedding themselves in a welter of leaves and stem.

'You never said,' she told him. She'd watched all this with an odd calmness and a feeling that this time things might turn out differently. As the flakes of fish had fallen like a snowstorm, she hadn't even felt annoyed. She could imagine her mother crying, 'Oh my God, what a terrible mess! Who's going to clean it all up?'

'And leeks too,' he shouted. He stood up, pulled his chair back from the table as if to make room for what was about to happen next. 'You always cooked leeks and I never ever liked them.'

'Leeks?' she said, as if acquainting herself with the word for the first time, 'leeks?' Something in her manner goaded him further.

'Leeks, I'm telling you, leeks. You're a rotten cook, rotten. Any fool can cook, any fool can read a recipe book and find out how to cook a decent meal, but you...'

'I haven't noticed you trying.' The calmness had given way to a feeling of inevitability, a secret knowledge that the things they were going to say to each other were going to hurt and could never be taken back and wrapped up again. Like unsuitable presents, they could not be exchanged for something else. A small evil voice inside her said: at last. She could not have said how long they'd been spoiling for a row, positively avoiding one, protecting themselves from certain destruction. She'd try to keep her mouth shut.

'Can you hear me?' he shouted, 'are you even listening?' His stance became more aggressive. Though he'd never hit her, she could not have guaranteed that he never would. He flung his arm out in a flailing motion that shocked her with its primitiveness.

She said, 'I'm listening but I don't really care for what I'm hearing.' She paused, uncertain whether to press her point, then took a deep breath and went on, 'I don't like to be shouted at, you know that. I can't bear it. It just makes me...' She spread out her hands. But he paid no attention.

'You're so stupid, woman. You never remember anything. Brain the size of a pea.' She realised that there was no going back, and wondered if her neighbours could hear him. She decided that she didn't care – she'd listened to them quarrelling often enough.

Without warning he came round the table and lunged at her with his left arm. She could see flakes of fish stuck in his greying hair and she stifled a desire to laugh. She wanted to shield her face and protect herself from the blows by running away. But this was not the time to run away. This time she must stay. She heard a car passing the house. It sounded much farther away than usual. The white digital clock on the wall blinked to 1.20.

When he lunged at her again, she stepped back and he fell sideways bumping against the table. He straightened up and retreated, unabashed.

'Eternal fish,' he was saying now, as if he were talking to himself, saying something aloud that he had prepared long ago.

'Life doesn't begin and end with fish,' he told her.

'I was testing a new recipe,' she said. Why was she trying to justify herself to him? It was pointless. There was no reason, no reason at all except that she had once been in love with him, they had been in love with each other. How could she ever have loved this lunging ape? All the feelings that she had been bottling up for so long came flooding into her mind and she longed to shout them out, cursing him and all his shortcomings. It took a strength she hadn't even been aware of to swallow all these old hurts and say instead, 'What's the matter with you today?' The question seemed innocent enough but as soon as she'd asked it, she knew she'd said the wrong thing.

'Matter? What's the matter?' He spat at her, standing up straight and rocking on his feet, as if he were trying to get his balance back. Now he was close to her and she could feel his stale breath on her cheek. She turned her head sideways to avoid it. The tension between them tightened and tightened. He turned away and addressed the room as if it were an audience.

'What's the matter, she wants to know? What's not the matter? Can anything ever go right, anything at all?'

She sighed, a deep sigh that reached to the pit of her stomach. She stepped back from him as she might have done from a wayward horse. This was his ranting phase. Better to let him get on with it than try to answer back or make excuses for herself. She had done it often enough but lately she'd learnt that there was no point in trying to make him see reason. Sweet reason, now she understood why they called it sweet. Button your lip, her father would have said. Her tongue thickened in her mouth until it seemed to fill all the available space. He was ranting about how miserable she made him, what a travesty their life together had been, how their children had deserted them because she'd harried them so much. She knew it all by heart, could have recited it with him. She closed her eyes for a second and wondered how she could make a phone call without distracting his attention, without damming up the flow.

She should have realised it would be like this, she should have arranged to give them some sort of signal. She took the kettle off the cooker and filled it under the tap, set it on the gas. Now that the time had come, she was not sure she could go through with it. Earlier she had told herself, the very next time it happens, I shall have him taken away. I have to do it. For my sake, for the children's. Perhaps they would come back. She looked out of the window at the quiet suburban view of back gardens. Somewhere out there they were grown up and going on with their lives.

After a few minutes the shouting petered out. When she didn't reply, he had nothing to urge him on. She looked at his eyes. The pupils had enlarged and darkened into black orbs in the paleness of his long narrow face.

'Have a cup of tea,' she said, 'it'll do us both good.' For answer he snatched a plate from the rack and threw it at her. But he had never been a sporting man and his aim was not good. The plate bounced on the counter beside her, spun round but didn't break. She put out her hand and checked its movement. He was off again on a monologue of her faults. Carefully she edged away. She took down the red enamel teapot. The kettle had never taken so long to boil. She heated the pot and placed two Earl Grey teabags in it. He began to shout again. Sweat glistened at his temples. When this had first happened, she'd expected that the fit would pass, that he'd run out of steam if she remained calm. She heard the words strewn together in phrases, sentences, but she didn't let their meaning enter her understanding. She hoped against hope that he wouldn't touch her. Though they were light years apart, the space between them was small.

The kettle was boiling at last.

'I'm going to make us some tea,' she said in the same slow tone, the voice she would have used to a naughty child. She made the tea, took two mugs from the shelf. The mugs looked unfamiliar to her, as if she were seeing the blue willow pattern for the first time. She slipped past him, as if skirting a monument, to get to the fridge. She took out a carton of milk, edged past him again. He was standing with his eyes open, not seeing. She opened the carton and poured milk into the mugs. The fragrance of the tea floated up to her. She sugared one of the mugs, took a spoon from the drawer, stirred the tea.

She looked at him. His eyes bulged in his head and his face

was livid. His arms had stopped flailing and had fallen uselessly by his side.

'Tea?' Her voice sounded alien to her, as if it came from far off. His hand reached forward for the mug that she pushed towards him and she readied herself to duck in case he threw it at her. But she saw with surprise that his face was less contorted, he had relaxed a little. She took a long deep breath.

'Why don't you sit down?' she said. He obeyed her, sat on the chair she pointed to. Now was her chance. She took her mug in her hand and sipped from it. The tea watered her throat like a river flowing in the desert. She put the mug down and calculated her next move. She would give him something to eat. She reached down a biscuit tin with an old-fashioned picture with a pair of skaters on it. She opened the tin and passed it to him, always careful not to make any sudden jerky movement. He took two biscuits and began to eat them at the same time. She backed slowly out of the kitchen. As she moved past him, her hands itched to touch his shoulder but she held back. No, she told herself, no. Not when you have got this far.

Once out of the kitchen, she ran into the sitting room and closed the door. She picked up the phone and dialled a number. She didn't have to look it up, after all this time it was burnt into her brain. She could hear the buzz of the ringing tone being repeated over and over again. Inside her head, she screamed, answer the bloody phone, answer it! Finally somebody did.

'Dr. Gilbert?' she whispered. 'This is Mrs. Elliott. It's my husband. He's having an attack.' For a moment she had not known how she would describe it, what words she would use. 'If you could come as soon as possible.'

'Where exactly are you?'

'We're at home, in the kitchen.' Her mind engineered pictures of gleaming knives, spotless surfaces punctuated with blood, but she closed her eyes tight and continued, 'I'll leave the back door open for you.'

'We'll be there in a matter of minutes.' He rang off.

She felt dazed, weakened by the audacity, the finality, of her action. Her eyes focused on a print on the opposite wall but she could not have said what she saw. There was a sharp green smell from the bowl of hyacinths at her elbow. She returned the phone to its cradle. Now she had to go back. In there. She went into the downstairs cloakroom and flushed the loo. She slipped sideways through the kitchen door.

    He was still sitting at the table, staring at his left hand as if he had never seen it before, exploring its shape. His tea was still beside him, undrunk. She sat down at right angles to him. She couldn't bring herself to sit opposite him, to look him straight in the eye. Remorse, pity, all the emotions churned in her. For a moment she thought she might faint. The wall clock blinked its Cyclops eye to 1.40. She picked up her mug and drank.

Watching

He's just come out of his house and he's standing on his porch, the funny man, sizing up the day. He's wearing a dark grey suit with a waistcoat, a white shirt and a tie, looking as if he's about to take the train to work. The porch of his house is much bigger than a normal porch, in fact it's more like a portico, one of those things they have in country houses. A coach and horses could drive into it so that no one got wet when entering the house. The funny man's portico has four columns supporting it. It really looks like a Greek temple to me, with that little triangular bit of roof on top. It took him a long time to build the whole thing and as usual, he never finished it.

He stands there for a few minutes, looking up at the sky. He licks his index finger and holds it up to see if there's any wind but it looks calm this morning, a still autumn day. Then he goes back indoors again. Soon he reappears in overalls, a torn brown shirt, a dusty cap and a pair of old army boots tied up with string. He doesn't look like the same person. I'd call him crazy myself but my mother is embarrassed by words like crazy or mad and she calls him the funny man. From where I lie, downstairs in the front room (I can't get up and down now so Mother has moved my bed into her sitting room) I have a ringside view of the funny man and most of his activities. It is awkward for Mother having her sitting room filled up with my bed – the sofa and chairs have been pushed back to make space for it – and her Thursday afternoon bridge circle doesn't meet here any more.

    I don't get too bored lying here. As long as the funny man is working on his house, there is plenty to see. Watching him, I feel as if I'm doing something myself. It's much better than reading a book. Mother has just brought me breakfast but I've been awake since dawn. The doctor said I could have pills to make me sleep but I told him not to bother. If I take any more pills, I think I will just pop open like a pea pod with a row of pills inside.

    The man opposite gets up about seven o'clock, I think. Whether he has an alarm clock or wakes up by himself, I couldn't say. Around seven he opens his curtains and looks towards the east where the sun is rising. I can't see the sun but I can tell it's there as the yellow light spills over, like the yolk of my breakfast egg, and turns the funny man's house a honey colour. My mother always cooks me an egg for breakfast.

    'Strong enough to sit up and take a lightly boiled egg,' she says to me every morning. This is her way of letting me know that I should be getting better. If only I knew how. The doctor only comes twice a week now. I get the feeling that he's given me up for lost or maybe he just can't face Mother. She always looks at him in that imploring way like a dog waiting for someone to throw him a bone. She can't see, Mother, she doesn't want to understand. It's not anyone's fault, it just happened.

    This morning I try to eat my egg but I can't. It runs down the side of the shell and onto the Beatrix Potter egg cup I've had since I was small. I abandon the egg. I can't see the funny man, he's at the back of his house. You can never tell what he'll do next. Last week he was putting pebbledash on the front wall of his house. First he smoothed cement down the walls – he always mixes his own cement, I can see he loves doing that. Then he took a shovelful of pebbles from a bucket and launched them against the wall like a discus thrower. More fell off than stuck on and some of the cement flaked off too. I laughed quite a lot as I watched him. But he kept on and on at it all day until there were fewer and fewer gaps between the pebbles. About five o'clock he stood back to admire his handiwork. He was nodding his head and rubbing his hands together and I'm certain he was saying to himself, you've done a good job there. I would, if it were me.

I try to swallow my toast. I like drinking tea in the morning because the long nights make me thirsty but even when I cut the toast into minute pieces, I still can't get them down. I feel as if I am eating the paving stones the funny man laid in his front garden this summer. When I was able to walk about more, it was easier. I used to put all the stuff I couldn't eat in the bottom of the wardrobe and empty it all in the dustbin when Mother was out. Now I can hardly get out of bed any more, except when she helps me to the bathroom, so I just have to leave things on my plate. This upsets her. She looks at my plate and then at me with despair or the nearest thing to despair that she's ever going to reveal in my presence. In the same way that she pretends that the funny man is normal, Mother likes to pretend that I am going to get better. For years she pretended that my father had just gone away on a trip and that he would be coming back some day. That's just the way she is.

'You have to keep your strength up,' she says to me in a bright strangulated voice every time she takes away my tray. I'd like to take her gently by the shoulders and say, 'Mother when I die, it won't be the end of the world,' but I know that for her it will be. She's got no one except me, ever since my father went away. We don't hear from him but I think he sends money through a solicitor.

What I'd really like Mother to do now is to tidy up my bed, plump up the pillows and go out to do her shopping so that I can watch him in peace. He's round at the side of the house, mixing cement again. I can't see properly from here. One afternoon last spring they delivered a spiral staircase all in one piece to his house. I was still able to walk around then so I sat in the garden, quite fascinated, while he cemented it into place. He had already dug a sort of foundation for it but it was still quite a job. Now he can go up and down to the roof without having to mess up the inside of his house. Just as well, really, for now he's carrying the cement up there. Six times he goes up and down with the bucket and makes a pile of wet grey cement. It's not easy for me to see because along the front and right hand side of the roof he has built a little wall with crenellations like you have on a castle. In some places he's even put gunports! I hope he never intends to shoot out of them because I'll be straight in the firing line. I told Mother he had put up the spiral staircase so that he could make a quick getaway after sniping at the neighbours but she didn't think it was funny.

Now he is carrying planks up to the roof, along with a saw. The wood is unwieldy to carry and bangs on the metal rails of the staircase. He has never bothered to paint them so they have gone rusty and bled into the ground below. On the roof he's measuring something and then sawing up the planks. I sit bolt upright in bed but I still can't see properly. It was easier to see from the bedroom window but Mother got tired of running up and down the stairs. In a way, I feel closer to normal life down here. I can see people passing in the street (when I'm not too busy watching the funny man) and hear my mother working in the kitchen. I like to smell her bread and cakes cooking even though I'm not up to eating them.

On the other side of the house he's built two flying buttresses. I know that's what they're called because I looked them up in a book that Mother got for me. It's a book about architecture – that's where I found the word crenellations – and I needed it to work out what he was up to. He used to build houses for people before his wife died and he started adding all these bits to his own place. I can't wait to see what he's going to do next. He's taken his toolbox up there and he's trying to make some kind of box. It's about six feet long and it looks absurdly like a coffin. But it can't be. No one would make a coffin on the top of a house. I'd like to get out of bed and fetch the binoculars from the drawer in the hall but I don't feel strong enough. Besides Mother would have a fit if she came back from the shops and found me out of bed. I have to really stretch out to see. He has sawn about ten pieces of wood the same length – say about two feet long. Then he's got these other pieces, all different lengths. Talk about a puzzle – I can't make out what he's going to do with them.

It's exciting, watching him up there on the roof, even though it's giving me a pain in my neck. The other two sides of the roof, where there are no crenellations, he has already filled in with a balustrade. I like that, it's really elegant. He bought the pillars ready made. They're copied from Regency houses, I think. I love the short stubby columns, they look like a line of fat women with pitchers on their heads, walking to the well, especially when the sun is setting behind them.

I dropped off to sleep there for a few minutes. It's so quiet here when Mother has gone out. It's always good to wake up again though. People often talk about how horrible waking up is, how awful they feel, but I always feel great. At least I know I'm alive for a bit longer. I don't have to get up and go to school though, much as I'd like to.

Mother has brought me lunch – sole, mashed potatoes and peas. The peas are the only colour on the plate, a mushy green. I wish I could give it all to the funny man, he looks as though he could do with a good hot meal after all that hammering and sawing and running up and down the spiral staircase. He doesn't cook any proper meals, I'm certain. Mother did take him over some stews and pies after his wife died, but he didn't want them, she said. She was sad. She never says, no one eats my cooking, but I know that's what she's thinking. There's no way I can eat this lunch, well maybe a few forkfuls of mashed potato. There's nothing to wash it down with, only a glass of milk. I know it's calcium and good for the bones but I've never liked milk.

I've just figured out (I think) what the funny man is building on his roof – it's a staircase! That box construction was for the first step, the one on which all the others will rest. It runs about five feet in from the parapet. He's building it beside the balustrade but it can't be another staircase going up the side of the house, for one thing there isn't any room, what with the flying buttresses and all. So just where is this staircase going to go? I'll just have to wait and see. I worked it all out on a piece of paper. The two foot long timbers are for making the actual steps, the irregular ones are for the sides, each pair shorter than the next. There should be about ten steps, say six inches high, so that means the top one will be five feet higher than the roof! I've got so excited, my breath is coming in gasps.

Mother is cross when she comes in and finds me sweating.

'What have you been doing? You feel as if you have a fever. If you keep on like this, I shall have to get the doctor.'

Oh, no, I groan to myself, all he can do is give me more pills. Mother fetches a face towel soaked in cold water from the bathroom and sponges my forehead with it. She asks me, more gently, if I would like a cold drink.

'No thank you,' I tell her. I don't point out to her what the funny man is doing. She likes to pretend that he doesn't exist. Sometimes she breaks out and threatens to complain to the council about him, she's sure he hasn't got planning permission for any of this but I always beg her not to. There is a very good reason for this but I couldn't actually explain it to her in words. Sometimes I struggle through my pain, taking more pills than I care to, just for the pleasure of watching the funny man. It's too depressing for my school friends to come and see me now, they'd rather be out playing football or going swimming than visiting a wasted shrunken person who can't even get out of bed.

My only real friend these days is Katharine. She'll be here in a moment. She's a nurse who comes to give me a bedbath every afternoon at three. She has soft red hair pulled up out of sight under her cap and brown eyes like a spaniel I once had. Her apron makes a bristling sound as she walks. I'm not sure what age she is but she doesn't seem to be much older than I am. We talk about the funny man and what he's been doing all morning. Sometimes we talk about death. How it's not as bad as it seems. How it can relieve you from pain. I was glad when she started coming here about three months ago. Mother can't bear to see me getting thinner and thinner. When I lie down I seem to feel my bones sticking through my skin. Katharine is very gentle, she makes small deft movements like a bird. She would be so much better than the funny man at building a house. She wouldn't leave everything half finished as he does. Sometimes he works on a project for a morning and then forgets about it – in the afternoon he will start measuring to see what he could add on somewhere else.

I point out to Katharine the new project on the roof.

'I think it's a staircase,' I tell her, 'it's going to take a lot of cement. He carried up six buckets this morning and another six this afternoon.'

'He's a glutton for punishment,' she says and laughs. Her eyes dance when she laughs. I don't often see people laugh these days, certainly not my mother. Katharine puts a basin of hot water on the table beside my bed and rolls up her sleeves. Then she unfolds a clean yellow towel and places it on the bed.

'I bet you he won't finish this staircase,' I say.

'I bet you he will.'

'What do you bet me?'

'What would you like?'

Her hands massage me gently with the flannel.

'A game of Scrabble maybe?'

I'd like to ask her if she could come round next Sunday afternoon but it seems unfair, it's her only day off. Sunday afternoons seem to stretch out for weeks.

'I've got to go on somewhere today but I could stay another day.'

'We'll have to wait and see if he finishes it first. Where can he be building it to?'

Katharine rinses the flannel and crosses to the other side of the bed. It's a tight squeeze between it and the sofa.

'I think it's a stairway to heaven,' she says, giggling, her light cool hands on my back. After she has washed me and tidied up my bed, I always feel better. When mother changes the sheets, she makes such a fuss, I begin to know the meaning of the word bedlam.

The funny man has worked all day without a break and just as

Katharine arrived, he stopped and rushed off down the spiral stairs. He is probably in his kitchen now making himself a sandwich and a cup of coffee.

'He must be hungry after all that work,' Katharine says, 'I'm always ravenous by midday.'

I like the way Katharine talks to me. She doesn't try to spare my feelings and avoid certain subjects like other people do. She finishes tucking in my sheets. I don't say anything. I'm so comfortable now, just the right temperature with my pillows arranged carefully that I could fall asleep for a little while until the funny man comes back. Katharine blows me a kiss.

'See you tomorrow,' she whispers and slides out of the room, carrying the basin of water.

I sleep. I dream. I dream that I am working with the funny man, helping him to build a staircase which goes up and up into the sky until it is out of sight. He is not so scary when you work with him. He has a pleasant foxy face but his eyes glitter like marbles. Suddenly he turns into my father. He is staring at me as if he had never seen me before. I thought I had forgotten my father's face but there he is in my dream. I begin to talk to him but he turns away, he doesn't seem to hear me.

When I wake up it is after four. He is back on the roof but he's forgotten to put his cap on, a sure sign (to me anyway) that he's taken it off to eat. He covers the spread of concrete with the board he has cut. He can't do any more today, he has to leave the step to harden. He tidies up what remains of the cement and puts it in the bucket. He goes downstairs again – I feel tired just watching him – and fetches a tarpaulin from behind the house. He spreads it over the cement and anchors it with two planks. Then he sits down on the construction and smokes a cigarette. He looks pleased with himself. Work is over for the day a little earlier than usual. Now he'll go into the house, get cleaned up and come out wearing corduroy trousers and a tweed jacket with holes in the elbows. Clothes fit for a jumble sale, my mother says.

She's been upstairs cleaning the windows and now she comes

Watching

down to clean mine. I don't mind her being in the way as I know what the funny man will do next. He will take a basket and go to the shops. He spends quite a long time in the town so I think he might take a walk too. When the windows are finished, the sharp lemony smell of the cleaning fluid cuts through the air. Mother brings me a cup of tea which I accept gratefully. Watching the funny man is a thirsty occupation. I think of all the cement and sawdust he must have breathed in up there on the roof. Maybe he's gone to the pub for a pint.

Now Mother is in the kitchen, rattling pots and pans. She's always so busy. I turn on the radio. Soon it will be time for another dreaded tray. In the evenings though, she usually brings me soup and a milk pudding. I can manage both if the soup has not got too many bits in it and the pudding isn't lumpy tapioca which sticks in my throat. The funny man has come back from his shopping, I think. It's a pity I can't see his kitchen from here, then I would know a lot more about him. I would like to know what he has for supper, does he have chips and fish fingers? At seven he comes into his living room and switches the television on. If I pull myself up in bed I can see the flicker of it. Mother bought me a little TV set but it makes my head ache, so I don't watch it often. I like to listen to the radio and read my book. After supper, when she's done the washing up, Mother will come and play cards with me. The evenings are very long. Mother draws the curtains so I can't see what time he goes to bed. When I was upstairs in my bedroom, his light used to go off round midnight.

I hope the cement is drying well, that it won't rain and that he'll be able to continue tomorrow. Just as I am at last dropping off to sleep, I wonder if the funny man will go on to construct some marvellous building some day, like Notre Dame or the Taj Mahal. Or maybe even a ziggurat, there is a picture of one in the book. But really, I think I would like to walk up his staircase to heaven if he ever gets it finished in time.

*Close Your Eyes
Little Sister*

Jason is my passion. He comes up behind me and says, 'Close your eyes, little sister,' and then he puts his arms around my neck and kisses me on the ear. His lips are as soft and sweeping as the ostrich plumes on Mother's pink hat.

I can't get used to the idea that I have no parents, that I'm not tied down any more. I feel as if they have gone away on a holiday though they hardly ever did. I'm not supposed to be here at all. The aunts think I'm staying with my friend Anne in Surrey. I always liked her at school but she's changed. She's dyed her hair blonde and she finds me dull, I can tell. She's only interested in boys and when I was staying with her, I was a liability, always dragging along behind, waiting to see what would happen. Would she kiss them, would she do the things with them that I do with Jason?

No one but Anne and Jason know I'm here. Anne was so relieved when I left, she promised she wouldn't tell. She sends on my letters without letting her mother see them. Yesterday I took the train down to Surbiton to post a letter to the aunts. I hate writing letters but these ones are easy to make up. I tell them that we are going cycling and having picnics. As the train crawls out of London, it reminds me of the funeral.

Aunt Isa and Aunt May. I can see them sitting in their

drawing room. Mother said it hadn't been changed since their grandmother's day and could have been turned into a museum. It's a dark room, dark blue wallpaper, little vases and brass pots and plants everywhere, rather like you were under the sea. They mean well, the aunts, but when I stayed with them after the funeral, it was suffocating. Even going to tea with Aunt Heather provoked a long discussion about what to wear. Once they were talking about weddings and Aunt Isa said, 'Myrtle got married in green and look what happened to her!' Then she looked at me and changed the subject. I didn't say anything. I just wondered.

I wonder about so many things. Why was Mother always so unhappy? I thought married people were supposed to live happily ever after. Jason said no, they'd grown apart. I didn't understand what that meant, it sounded like two trees growing in different directions. When Father and Mother argued, the atmosphere would be jagged black for days. When they weren't speaking to each other, it made it easier for me, sometimes (though very rarely) I could ask Father for something without Mother finding out.

Jason phones me late at night. He is in the Middle East somewhere, he works for a petrol company. We have long talks. Sometimes we imagine what we'll do with the money but in the end we may not do anything special. There are a few things I would like. Mother always wanted to go to China but Father said it would be ridiculous to travel so far and eat such ghastly food. She took to playing bridge in the afternoons. She said to me once, 'I hate playing bridge and I despise the people who play it,' in that short little voice of hers and then she got into her car and drove away to her bridge party.

The day the accident happened, Anne and I were finishing our exams. When we came out of the exam room, we went into the loo and cried, we were so certain we'd done badly. We cried so hard that we made ourselves laugh and then we became hysterical. I wasn't able to cry at all when they told me about the accident. I haven't cried since.

Jason is supposed to look after me until I come of age next

year. He says if I behave sensibly, I can do what I like. I'm not used to doing what I like. Mother always wanted me to do what she wanted, what she considered right and proper. Now I do lots of things that Mother would never have allowed. I rarely wash the dishes. I have fry ups every night, very bad for your skin, I can hear her saying. I eat butter and marmalade on my toast and I never cut off the crusts. Every night I have some chocolate cake – it's so comforting when I'm alone.

I'm not used to being alone. I stand at the kitchen window in the dark and watch the people in the flats opposite and wish I were over there with them. There are more noises in the flat at night than I ever noticed before. Creaks and bumps and whispering. When I feel frightened, I think about Jason and being in his arms and I'm OK. I dunk biscuits in my coffee and drop crumbs all over Mother's Chinese rug. There is no one to say, 'You shouldn't do that, Felicia,' in that accusing little voice. No one, no one at all. It's as if a heavy weight has been lifted from the back of my neck, like when I took my satchel off when I got home from school. Now I don't have to worry about school or the exam results or what I'm going to do next year.

Today I went to Harvey Nichols. I couldn't see anything I liked so I went to Harrods. I wanted a cup of coffee but they said it was too late, nearly lunchtime, so I had a frozen yoghurt instead. It was rather good, all smooth and slippery, much better than ice cream. Mother would have said that I was spoiling my lunch. She loved Harrods Food Hall. She was not a greedy person but she always bought something to eat there. Some of those little Viennese pastries or some croissants or some handmade chocs. She didn't care for the rest of the store, she said there were far too many tourists there these days. Sometimes she'd come upstairs with me to look at clothes if it was a good day.

I never knew when the good days or the bad days would be. On the bad days Mother would wake up in a dark mood which seemed to get darker as the day wore on. She would go out to lighten the blues, as she called it, and that would help. She would take a taxi to Knightsbridge and if it was the school holidays I would have to go with her. She would fret and fret when we were stuck in a traffic jam in Park Lane. The cars there, she said, were like lemmings rushing towards the edge of a cliff at the bottom of which was south London. People didn't go south of the Thames, if they could help it, she told me. I wonder what she'd think of Anne now, her family moved to Surbiton the day after the summer holidays started.

I feel sorry about leaving Anne's house even though her mother was so determined that I should be sad.

'Poor Felicia,' she'd say when I came down for breakfast. Even though I didn't want it, she insisted on cooking me bacon and egg and sausage. I hate greasy food in the mornings and I couldn't eat it.

'Poor Felicia,' she'd say again, looking at Anne who was stuffing her face with cornflakes, 'she hasn't got her appetite back yet.'

All I wanted was some dry brown toast and coffee though it reminded me of Mother on her bad days. She'd drink nothing except a cup of black coffee, then she'd take off for the shops. Sometimes she wouldn't get back until after I'd got home from school and she'd be laden with shopping. She'd pull the clothes out of the bags and try them all on, talking all the time, her eyes bright with excitement. That was the only thing that ever seemed to cheer her up. Then she would put them away in the wardrobe. She hardly ever wore them – Mrs. Calloway had the best of them.

I sleep in Mother's room with the windows open. She never opened the windows at night – she was afraid of moths and she worried that a bat might fly in and get caught in her hair, her long chestnut hair, and that she'd have to have it all cut off. Did I believe that? I think I did but not now. I've read lots of articles in the newspapers lately which said that bats are quite harmless. I've taken Mother's pink and blue eiderdown off the bed and replaced it with my old green one. It smells of mothballs from being shut up in the cupboard. She bought me a new one but I never used it. The first night the mothbally smell kept me awake but now I've got used to it.

I stretch out on the bed and turn the end of the eiderdown in underneath my feet. I haven't slept in my own room for ages. They put up a new light on the fire escape and it shone into my room and kept me awake, so I went into Jason's room to sleep. I fixed my pillow and bolster to make it look as if I were asleep in my own bed.

Jason had two beds in his room in case he had a friend to stay in the holidays. He didn't mind me sleeping there. When he left school and went to university, he was at home much more often and I used to talk to him for hours. I always went back to my own room before Mother got up and she could never understand why I was so tired in the morning. I told her I stayed up late studying. She never guessed. If she wasn't going out to some boring dinner, Mother would take her Mogadon soon after supper. She'd come in and kiss me good night as I sat in my room doing homework.

'Don't stay up too late, darling,' she'd say, 'I'm just going to read my library book for a little while.' As she drifted into her room, she'd release her long shining hair from its pleat. Father would be in his study at the other end of the flat. I never noticed what time he went to bed.

Jason and I always giggle a lot. He said what we were doing was wrong but I couldn't see why. He told me that men and women do it, even Mother and Father, but not brothers and sisters. At first I didn't believe him, it couldn't be the same thing, it must be different. I couldn't describe the ecstasy of it to anyone, not even to Anne. The girls at school talked about it all the time but not about their own brothers. They were always swopping clothes and going to parties at the weekends. I was often invited but Mother would never let me go, she said I couldn't return the invitation and after a while people stopped asking me.

'It's no use asking Felicia, her silly parents won't let her do anything,' they'd say. On Mondays they would get together in corners and talk about the party and giggle just like Jason and me.

Our weekends were always the same. Aunt Isa and Aunt May came to tea on Saturdays. Aunt Isa's teeth clicked when she was eating her cake. Aunt May would be cross because Isa had woken her out of her afternoon nap. Aunt May's hair was short and grey and hung in little wisps over her forehead like a dog's. Isa wore hers in this tremendous pompadour, all rolled and curled. When I was little I used to wonder if she went to sleep like that and if rats ran in and out of her hair like they said they did in olden times. I didn't dare ask Mother, she would have clutched her own hair and screamed at the mention of rats.

A man followed me round the V and A today. He watched me all the way through Textiles. There are hardly ever any men in Textiles, I suppose because it's too domestic for them, though you do see them in the dress section. I like looking at the lace and embroidery and thinking about the people who made them. There's a pair of socks knitted in the fourth century. How can they still be there with no holes or darns when Mother and Father are gone?

I didn't like the look of this man. He was small and bald and his head was bent over on one side like a flower that's broken off its stem. His shirt was grubby. I thought he was going to flatten me between the big display panels in there, squash me flat like a pressed flower in one of Mother's books. He kept on pulling the panels in and out as if he were looking for something but all the time he was watching me with beady black eyes.

Mother always went on about men, how I shouldn't do anything to encourage them or sit beside them on the bus or the tube if I could help it. She used to go on and on until I stopped listening. Father would say sometimes, 'Oh you do exaggerate, Myrtle!' and she would cry, 'What do you know about it, Arnold, you're not a woman?' If I ever had to come home late at night, I was to take a taxi, she would pay. Now I walk in the dark. I've never been allowed to, only home from the bus stop. The lights colour the trees an unnatural lime. I walk through streets I've never seen by night, a whole new country.

On the way home from Harrods I went to McDonald's. Mother hated junk food. I had a hamburger and a chocolate milkshake. I ate the hamburger walking along the street. Mother didn't approve of eating in the street. Eating must be done indoors sitting down, unless it was a picnic. I drank the milkshake on the bus. When I sucked up the last drops, the straw made a sound like the sea sucking over pebbles. 'Enjoying your drink?' the bus conductor asked.

'Yes,' I answered him, surprised. He was a large wide man with hair the colour and texture of crinkle cut chips which I've taken to eating recently. He waved when I got off the bus and I waved back. I threw the empty carton in the canary yellow waste bin by the bus stop. I really felt like throwing it on the ground but there were too many people around, I didn't dare.

'Oh, I am being very bad and naughty,' I told Jason on the phone last night. 'I called Aunt Isa and told her that I was staying another week at Anne's.' He just laughed at me.

'That's not my idea of wickedness,' he said. Then he said the flat needed to be cleared of their belongings, and that I should make a start. Otherwise, he said, the aunts will come over and fight like harpies over Mother's things. I don't know what to throw away. All Mother's clothes? All Father's books? I think I'll wait for Mrs. Calloway to come back. That's the kind of thing she'd love to do. Jason will be home next week. We'll be alone in the flat. It won't be the same without Mother and Father, we won't have to be quiet. We can have all the doors open if we like, we can have midnight feasts and sing in the bath.

I've done so many of the things that Mother told me not to do and nothing has happened to me. Perhaps she should have done the things she wanted to do. The aunts were just as bad, trying to get me to behave. Why didn't they want me to have any fun? Jason used to get into terrible scrapes. He never did what anyone told him. He used to tell me about the tricks he'd played on people at school, things I would never have dreamed of doing, and then we'd giggle.

I'll have to clear up before Jason comes. The sofa cushions are covered with little dots of melted chocolate, like the moles on Aunt May's cheek. The kitchen is beginning to smell. I shall buy Jason's favourite things, smoked salmon and those tiny little salamis and some white wine. He likes Muscadet. I'm not much good at cooking.

Mrs. Calloway never liked people messing up her kitchen. We can go to restaurants. I haven't been brave enough to go to a restaurant by myself yet. Yesterday I went to the National Gallery and queued in the basement for my lunch on a tray but that's not the same. Father used to take us to an Italian restaurant in St. John's Wood for Sunday lunch. He said it made up for having the aunts to tea on Saturday. I would have liked to have gone somewhere else for a change but Father liked routine. He liked to go to the office at the same time every day and read the Financial Times – pink – such an unsuitable colour for men. I always thought it should have been green.

Jason is coming, oh I can hardly wait. We can't even go to a pub, I am still under age. I look at myself in the mirror. Could anyone tell? I am wearing the new red dress I got at Brown's. I've had my hair cut. Mother always said a women's crowning glory is her hair but it was such a nuisance drying it. It's all short and curly now, I had it cut in Bond Street in this place I read about in Vogue. I felt strange and frightened when I went in, but even stranger when I came out with no weight hanging down my neck. On the way back, I thought this man was following me from the tube station. He was tall with a dark blue shirt. He had a hairy chest and pale hairy arms. He gave me the creeps. Jason has strong tanned arms.

Jason is coming tomorrow, hooray! I went down to Surbiton again this morning to post a letter to the aunts to keep them off my trail. I bought a postcard from the National Gallery for Aunt Heather and wrote it in the Post Office. I've done the washing up at last. What a pile there was. I've tidied the kitchen and washed the floor but it still has grey streaks on it. I hoovered Jason's room and Mother's room and the sitting room. No point in cleaning everywhere. I did some dusting too. I thought of all the ornaments in the aunts' drawing room while I was doing it. They won't be able to hassle me when Jason comes back, he is my legal guardian. I want everything to be perfect for him. I hope he likes my hair.

I am in the bath when he comes. I hear the door creak. I left it open for him.

'Jason,' I call, 'oh Jason, I'll be out in a minute.' I hear him clearing his throat and I jump out of the bath and wrap myself in one of Mother's best pink towels. I glance at myself in the mirror, my face is pink like the towel. I rush into the hall, saying, 'Jason, Jason,' in a soft voice as if I were calling a kitten. He is not there. He is hiding from me. I can't wait to see him. I feel his arms slide round my neck and I wait for his kisses.

'Oh Jason!' I cry. I open my eyes. But the arms are not Jason's. They are hairy like a monkey's and they tighten around my neck till I cannot breathe.

Alice's Pipistrelles

Aunt Alice's bats were famous. They were a special kind, called after her. Nobody could touch them or chase them out of her barn. There could be no loud noises that would alarm them. No rowdy parties either, not that she went in for that kind of thing. She was proud of this notoriety and people came from obscure nature programmes to record the bats squeaking. I was terrified of them and much as I loved Aunt Alice, it was difficult for me, after the bats became famous, to persuade myself to go and stay with her, as I did every holidays.

I was worried about headlines like Famous Bat Becomes Tangled in Teenager's Hair. My hair was not as long as Aunt Alice's but she pinned hers expertly into a chignon each morning, so I was more likely to get a bat tangled in mine. Ever since some kind of flying creature had got stuck in my hair when I was sleeping in Aunt Alice's spare room, I had a thing about finding creepy crawlies in it. I fabricated nightmares out of bluebottles and horse flies and long dead insects, the sort you see inside dusty shop windows. I imagined that their wings and bodies mingled with my hair and only disappeared when I washed them off down the sink. Extra protein I told myself but I didn't really believe it.

Of course Aunt Alice denied all this. When I said I could hear the bats squeaking at dusk and could smell their droppings on the evening breeze, she said she couldn't hear them at all because after a certain age, people could no longer hear higher frequencies. Dogs, she said, had much more acute hearing than people. I didn't ask her how she knew this, since she'd never had a dog. I knew she would give me chapter and verse and where to look it up in her library, even to the page and paragraph in the book. It was because she read books that I liked Aunt Alice, we often swapped stories. My mother thought books were a waste of time.

It was a shame about the barn because I used to play there with Tully on rainy days. I loved hiding in there among all the ancient farm machinery, the rotting leather of harnesses, their clinking metal when you brushed against them in the dark. It wasn't a scary place to me then but later I kept away from it. And I thought you got less scared as you grew up. Tully lived over the fields and I wasn't supposed to play with him. My mother thought he wasn't good enough for me because his father was a farmer. What an awful snob she was, my mother. There was hardly anyone in the county who was fit to speak to and the ones who were I hated. So there I was, hiding in the barn with Tully and loving every minute of it, just to spite my snobby mother. Aunt Alice didn't care, I was only expected to come home for meals. Our house was not far away but there was no view of the sea, and my mother was constantly asking what I was doing and where I was going. I preferred being at Aunt Alice's.

Now I was walking down the Manor Walk, through the stile and down the lane to the open land that gave on to the rocks and the sea. There had always been cows grazing there (I was afraid of them too) but half the land had been swallowed up by the second nine holes of the golf course, recently added. I walked along the edge nearest the beach, like a tightrope between the edge of the shorn grass and the rocks. I'd been walking here for ever. I could hear myself saying to anyone who challenged me, I have been walking across this land for fifty years, ever since my mother wheeled me here in a pram, and I'm not about to stop now. Would I have the nerve to say it if a bunch of burly golfers challenged me? It was too far to run back to the stile so I would have to carry on along this path to the Silver Strand which was just out of sight.

I climbed over more rocks and down an overgrown brambly path and there it was, one of the emptiest beaches in Inishowen. The last five summers I'd been here alone. I'd seen footprints but I'd never met anybody. I checked the round depression in the rocks where we used to spread our rug to keep out the keen summer breeze. I strolled to the place where I'd played café by myself. Sometimes I would admit others into this game but they were never as interested as me. There was a stool, a high stool, and a long counter and then a place where you went to get the ice cream before putting it in little silver dishes and carrying it to the customers. Only in my head of course. I stood there now and pretended I was doing it. Up on the promontory was a hotel where I was in charge, or else a cowboy ranch depending on what I felt like playing. I played up there for hours either rushing round on my horse or helping guests to settle in, putting up with their complaints, in my head making little rooms from the hollows in the heather and rocks.

I still would not admit to myself why I had come. Aunt Alice was long dead and so was my mother, laid cosily to rest in Ballybrack churchyard, under the green of the hill. The old house had gone, replaced by an enormous modern monstrosity with huge gables, dormer windows and a fancy picket fence all around it. It was painted a garish yellow ochre and looked more like Southfork than Inishowen. The barn was still there, surrounded now by a thick clump of trees.

The truth was, I wanted to see Tully. The other years I'd hesitated but now I wanted to see him. I wanted to see how he was, even though I knew he would be a gnarled bald old man like his father had been.

A tall man was walking across the grass towards me. He was wearing highly polished shoes, shining with dew, charcoal trousers, a hand-knitted sweater. He looked as if he belonged to the place. Should I ask him?

I lifted my eyes to his face. His eyes were very blue.
'Can you tell me if the bats are still there, in the barn?'
He stared at me. We both spoke at once.
'Are you?'
'It is, isn't it?'
I'd found him. I wanted to kiss him but it was far too soon. Or was it far too late?

I was far too young to fall in love with Tully, I was only about seven or eight when I started playing with him. I would run out of the house and meet him at the bottom of the Pollan field at the far end of the golf course. We would wander over the golf course, taking care not to walk in front of people who were driving from the tees. Then we'd play on the headland above the Silver Strand and sometimes climb right over the far side of it to a triangular beach with no name. It was only visible at low tide so the sand was always smooth and clean with no footprints. It was scary to stay too long on this beach for the tide would come in fast and leave us marooned – we had to climb back up through the slippery grass and rocks. But there was never anyone else there, which we liked.

When we were older we would sit down in a hollow on the headland. We held hands and laughed and told jokes. That was all there was to it. My mother said I was too old to be playing with boys. Was she mad? Too old? I was just getting to the age for boys. What she really wanted was to keep me under her thumb. That was when Tully and I graduated to the barn.

Later I was sent away to boarding school while Tully went to school in Moville. I saw him a few times after that, but we didn't really talk, just said hello. How could I ever have told Tully how I felt?

'The bats are still there,' he said. Now he was shy. Tully. Not like his dad, not squat and bald. How had he imagined me, I wondered, if he'd ever imagined me at all?

There was such a large gaping silence between us, I had to fill it.

'I was always scared of them, you know, I thought they'd get tangled in my hair and I'd have to get it cut off.'

Tully looked at my hair, now cropped and going grey and laughed.

'You wouldn't have to worry about that now.'

'No,' I said with regret.

'We could go and have a look, if you like.'

'Yes.' I was just as frightened as if I were eight years old again. I wouldn't be able to hear the bats squeak, I was too old. Older than Aunt Alice when I knew her first. She'd probably been in her forties then, which to me had been as old as Methuselah.

As I walked across the field beside Tully, I had a sinking feeling in my stomach. I told myself I was being ridiculous. I'd done it, I'd found Tully, I was walking along beside him! How could I be scared of a few old bats? Alice's Pipistrelles. I wondered how long they lived.

Wasn't this what I wanted? What I had planned, what I had thought about idly, on cold winter nights? Meeting Tully again. But I hadn't imagined any more than that. I hadn't thought of what I would say to him, or what would happen. It had only been a daydream.

Sandy McCready had wanted us to take part in the Young Cup for people under eighteen. He was one of Aunt Alice's beaux. He was a Scot with flaming red hair in crimped waves (I envied him that) and he wore peculiar clothes, like green trousers, a red shirt and a tan jacket. Tully and I sometimes got the giggles when we saw him on the golf course – he wore yellow plus fours over thick hand knitted socks. Sandy said to Aunt Alice, 'Why don't Ginny and her wee friend come and play in the Young Cup?' I can see now that he was desperate to prove himself to her.

Tully and I had never played golf, even though we walked over the golf course all the time. I thought it a boring game and I still do. His father played golf – he said the clubhouse was his nearest pub so he might as well play when he had the time. My mother thought this was preposterous – 'The cheek of the man,' she cried, 'he comes into the bar as bold as brass!' But she wanted me to play golf, I might meet the right kind of person – a future doctor or lawyer would have fitted the bill. What I wanted didn't come into consideration.

Sandy said there would be a bunfight afterwards. I didn't know what a bunfight was. Was it like a pillow fight, only people threw buns at each other? Aunt Alice explained that it meant tea, with sandwiches and cake. Sandy said he would provide us with a few clubs – we could both use the same ones and he would take us round the course and mark our cards. Tully and I spent a whole afternoon with him on Aunt Alice's back lawn, hitting balls, with Sandy scrutinising our swings. It looked easy but when I took the club in my hands and felt its heft, it was much heavier than I expected. It felt even heavier when I tried to raise it high in the air in a graceful ellipse and bring it down to hit the ball.

But we did sign up for the cup, donated by Archdeacon Daley and his wife, who also provided the sandwiches. There were lots of other children, accompanied by braying parents wearing two tone studded shoes with white laces. They were probably people my mother would have allowed me to speak to but I didn't like the look of them. Tully and I caught each other's eye and tried not to laugh. Sandy led us out onto the first hole. He propped up the ball on its tiny white tee. I wanted a coloured tee but I had to make do with the first one Sandy took from the pocket of his shapeless tan jacket. We drove the balls straight down the fairway. Beginners' luck. We started our slow plod round the course.

Mr. Anderson from Ballymagowan, with three dark haired boys in tow, caught up with us at the fourth hole. I said we should let them go on, but Sandy said we shouldn't give way to them. I don't remember how many balls we sliced – they just dropped sideways off the tee. When we did hit them they went into the rough grass. Behind us the boys fell about laughing. Mr. Anderson watched with a grin on his face as we walked down the slope to look for our balls.

We knew we were awful. At the fourth green I took six strokes just to get the ball near the hole. But Sandy was full of encouragement.

'Youse are grand, youse are going to win, I'm telling ye.'

We got to the clubhouse and handed the clubs back to him. We were hungry for the bunfight. When we got inside, we discovered that everyone else had finished ages ago and there were hardly any sandwiches left, only dog-eared fish paste ones and two tired pieces of sponge cake. Aunt Alice never cut cake into such small mean slices. I made a face at Tully, we took what was left and sat on the windowsill in a corner of the room. It was too noisy to hear yourself speak. The tea in the thick white cups was lukewarm. Not my idea of a party.

'Useless, isn't it?' I said into Tully's ear. He nodded.

'Complete waste of time.'

Nobody paid any attention to us. There was a hush as Archdeacon Daley stood up.

A spotty boy with glasses had won third prize. As he took the envelope he blushed so deeply that his spots disappeared. A handsome girl called Margaret with long pigtails was second and to our absolute amazement, Tully and I were declared joint first. Mr. Anderson, the man we'd met at the fourth tee, stared at us and then at Sandy who was standing at the bar, drinking whiskey. He said something out loud, but the Archdeacon quelled him with a look. Anderson walked over to Sandy and for a moment I thought he was going to strike him. He said something to Sandy who just shrugged.

I knew in my heart of hearts that it couldn't be true. We had played so badly, driven so many times into the bunker or the rough. I didn't dare look at Tully as we got up from the windowsill. The Archdeacon, smiling all over his broad face, put the cup into my trembling hands. I motioned to Tully to take hold of one of the handles and we held it up together. Nobody spoke. There was a very faint ripple of applause. I could see all those eyes levelled at me. We hadn't done anything wrong – Sandy had marked our cards and we didn't even know what he'd marked on them. He'd wanted us to win; he'd wanted to get into Aunt Alice's good books. How could he believe that he'd get around her by cheating? What on earth was I going to tell her?

Tully and I put the silver cup down on the table by the empty plates. We walked out of the clubhouse. We never played golf again.

Now Tully was taking me to the barn. I heard a lark trilling far above us, but when I looked up, I couldn't see it. The day was calm and bright but I was not calm. We walked along the boundary of the ugly ochre house. We were about twenty yards from the barn. It was dilapidated, but the roof had been repaired. I thought about the bats and ran my hand through my hair. I imagined it all fouled up with bats sticking to the tendrils. I stopped in my tracks, on the overgrown path beside the picket fence.

'Tully,' I asked, 'who owns the barn now? I mean should we be walking here?'

He stood still for a moment and smiled.

'I do,' he said. 'The rest of the land was sold to Ray McGann. But I bought the lot with the barn on it. He didn't want to have the responsibility of the bats.'

'You own it?'

'I thought I owed it to your aunt,' he said.

'You didn't owe her anything.' I was quite sure about this. Aunt Alice had always liked Tully.

'I couldn't let them get into the wrong hands, could I? And besides, they reminded me of you.' He was watching me.

'Like I said, I'm still scared of them,' I confessed.

'You're not, not really. Besides they'll all be asleep this time of day.'

'Will they? I can't remember.'

The ochre house was out of sight now behind the trees. The barn loomed in front of us.

'Do you think they're the same bats?' I said.

'How do you mean, the same?' Tully was puzzled.

'I mean, how long do they live? Are they the same ones that were here in Aunt Alice's time?'

'I haven't the slightest notion,' Tully said and laughed in his old way. Did I still laugh the same way, I wondered. Obviously my voice hadn't broken, but it might have changed its timbre. Was I fatter, was I fitter, had I remembered to put my make-up on? All of a sudden I needed to look in a mirror. I wanted to hold his hand the way I used to, when we sat on the triangular beach or in a hollow on the hill. But he was almost a stranger, I couldn't stretch out my hand to him. I knew very little about him. I'd never asked anybody who might know for fear of finding out something I didn't want to hear.

'Tully,' I said, as he unhooked the padlock on the door, 'are you…?'

But he couldn't hear me because of the rooks squawking in the trees behind us.

The door creaked open. I noticed how rusty the hinges were. I stood there in the sunlight. Inside it was very dark and I could see nothing.

'It's all right,' he said, 'there's nothing scary in there.'

I took a deep breath. There was a dry musty smell mingled with the acrid stink of the bat droppings.

'You didn't use to be scared of going in here with me, did you?' His blue eyes were fixed on my face. I went hot and cold.

'True,' I said.

Tully took my arm and pulled me inside the barn.

I thought of my life up to then. Luckily there was nobody to tell me how stupid I was, coming here every year, hoping to meet Tully.

The barn was dark and still. The bats were still up there on the beams but it was hard to see them in the gloom. Tully was so close I could feel the warmth of his body. I felt faint.

'Could we go somewhere and talk, d'you think?' he said as we turned to leave.

'Of course,' I said.

'I mean you aren't in a hurry or anything?'

I wasn't in a hurry to go anywhere, nobody was waiting for me, anywhere on earth.

As we reached the door, Tully took my hand and in slow motion, he drew me towards him and kissed me on the cheek. Then we kissed each other hard on the lips.

It was like coming back from the dead, when I'd been dead for centuries.

Tully stood back and eyed me doubtfully.

'Was that….?'

I breathed out and said, 'It was fine, Tully.'

'I mean I don't know what your circumstances are.'

'You don't know if I just escaped from a convent or whether I've been married three times.' I laughed and his eyes crinkled too.

'I don't know anything about you either,' I said.

Tully's eyes were less blue.

'My wife died. Five and a half years ago. Cancer.' He looked down at his shoes.

'I'm so sorry.' I touched his shoulder. 'My husband left me a long time ago. I have two daughters. Married. One in Canada and one in Australia.'

'We'll go to the clubhouse. Joe'll give us a drink.'

'Joe?'

'My cousin. He works there.'

'You haven't got any children?'

He shook his head, his face sombre.

I couldn't say I was sorry for that too, it might sound as if I was sorry for the whole life he'd led since I last saw him.

'So you're in charge of the bats now?'

We were walking down the path with sea in front of us. Cows were lowing in the distance.

'Yes. A man comes every year or so to check that I'm not mistreating them. I don't want to put up signs to keep people out, that would only attract them. So I don't paint the barn, I leave it looking all broken down.'

'Canny of you.'

'I wasn't canny enough though, was I?'

'How do you mean?'

I could smell the bitterness of the bright green ferns on the banks of the stream which ran down to the beach.

He reached over and took my arm again. It felt as if it were burning up.

'I should never have let you get away.'

'You make me sound like a fish – the one that got away.'

'No, no, that's not how I meant it.'

'I can't believe that I never knew you bought the barn.'

'I came to your aunt's funeral but you were too upset, I didn't want to bother you. I wanted to ask your permission…'

'You didn't need it,' I broke in. 'I just wanted rid of everything. Aunt Alice was more like my mother than my own mother was. If you follow my meaning.'

'I do indeed. Your Aunt Alice was a lovely woman. I go to her grave when I'm up there, in Ballybrack.'

'So it's you that lays the flowers?'

We smiled at each other.

We walked across the top of the beach, staring at the promontory. I was thinking about all the time we'd spent there together.

We crossed the putting green, after making sure there was nobody aiming for it.

The clubhouse was much bigger, a square modern building, not the prefab I remembered.

'Tully,' I said, just before we got there, 'do you remember what I said when I went away? I promised I'd come back and I never did…'

He turned to face me and put his arms round me.

'Let bygones be bygones? Besides I feel the bats belong to you.'

They were called after my aunt but how could bats belong to anybody?

I hugged him back and we walked into the bar. It was easier walking in there because it had changed so much.

'Do you remember the bunfight?' I asked Tully. He rolled his eyes to heaven.

'How could I ever forget?'

'Sandy never did any good with Aunt Alice. She knew he was a big fraud.'

'Would she have said the same thing about me, I wonder?'

'In what way were you a fraud?' I asked, sitting down at a table from where I could view the sea.

'You know…'

'No I don't.'

I believed that I was the fraud because I'd gone away to school and never had the courage to come back and tell Tully how I felt, even though I'd promised. Would I tell him now? There had to be a right time to say it.

Before I'd even decided what I wanted to drink, Tully came back to the table carrying a tray. On it were two glasses and a bottle of champagne.

'Tully! What's this in aid of?'

He put down the tray. He looked straight at me and said, 'You know perfectly well. Perfectly well.'

He picked up the bottle and tore off the foil.

'It's a pity we've wasted all this time,' he said, twisting the cork out. We smiled at each other as the champagne popped. He poured me a glass.

'But I don't intend to waste another minute.'

I nodded. We'd never had a drink together before, we'd been too young. I took my glass and he lifted his and we clinked.

'To the bats,' I said.

Tully laughed, showing his still good teeth. I thought he'd worn better than me but it didn't seem to matter.

'To us,' he said and sipped his champagne.

It was late when we came out of the clubhouse. There were only a few cars parked on the grass verge.

'Is your car here?' Tully asked.

'No, it's right up in the lane. I never park here, I like to walk all the way.'

He took my arm.

'I'll walk you there.'

'You don't need to…' I said.

'Of course I do.'

We walked all the way back. It seemed to take us about two minutes. We could hear the sea whispering on the Silver Strand. There was nobody on the beach, and only a few straggling golfers coming up to the putting green.

'You'll give me your phone number,' Tully said.

'You're not asking, you're telling me.'

'That's it, I'm not letting you get away till you give it to me.' This was Tully in a different guise, a Tully I'd never known, a man organising his life.

When we got to my car, I found a scrap of paper in my handbag and wrote my number on it. I took out my diary and wrote Tully's name and number on the back page.

'Where are you staying?'

'At a B & B. So you can't really phone me till I get home.'

His face darkened, the happiness drained from it.

'I'll phone you,' I said, 'if you like.'

The moment was approaching when I would say goodbye to Tully and words had deserted me. He drew me close to him. I felt as if I had at last come home. The thick marl of his sweater rubbed against my skin.

'Sorry about all this,' he said, 'I was just so surprised to see you.'

He stood back and looked at me.

'It was great seeing you,' I told him.

That night I lay awake in a strange bed in a strange room and looked upwards in the darkness. Meeting Tully again had been a great shock. I didn't know what to think, what to expect.

The next day, I parked the car in the same place and walked down the dark lane, through the trees. The wind was whipping the branches and the rain stung my face. Beyond the stile there were muddy pools where the cattle's hooves had churned up the earth. I

Alice's Pipistrelles

couldn't see the cows today. On the other side of the lough I couldn't see the mountain either. A sea fret made it look as if the water spread to infinity.

I made myself walk up the path towards the barn. I unhooked the padlock as Tully had, and edged my way inside. I remembered looking up pipistrelles in the dictionary when they were first discovered.

'Bats,' Aunt Alice had said. I thought pipistrelle was a beautiful word, much much nicer than bat. She thought they were cuddly creatures when we pored over the pictures in the Children's Encyclopaedia. 'Horrible!' I'd squeaked, 'they look like flying rats.' Aunt Alice had laughed. We decided that my mother would like them even less than I did.

I breathed in the sharp smell. It was not so unpleasant. This time I wanted to remember it. The bats were up there, above me, in a dark mass – I imagined I could hear their wings fluttering in the gloom and their high pitched squeaks.

'Adieu, adieu, Alice's Pipistrelles,' I whispered and turned to leave the barn. I could hear the rain hitting the corrugated iron roof. I took an envelope from my pocket and tucked it in behind the padlock.

The cows were cruising towards the stile, so I gave them a wide berth and walked fast so I could get there before them. My shoes were covered with mud but nothing worse. I twisted through the stile with relief. I looked back at the grass and the sea beyond it one more time. My suitcase was already in the car – I was going to drive away and never come back. I was a coward, I was running away. I had decided that it was too late for Tully and me.

He was sitting on the wall beside the car. I jumped when I saw him.

'Tully! You put the heart out of me.'
'I came to see you.'
I tried to make light of the situation.
'I didn't think you'd come to see the cows.' Tully said. He

walked towards me.

'Don't go away,' he pleaded. 'Please stay. Don't leave me again.'

'Yes,' I shouted, 'yes.' I didn't wish to argue.

And that was how I became the keeper of Alice's Pipistrelles.

The Two O'clock Train

Anne sat on the edge of her seat, willing the train to start. Her hands trembled. She stared at the other passengers. How could they just sit there – reading talking, looking out of the window – as if nothing had happened? On the phone her sister had said only that Hugh and the boys were in hospital. But she could guess. Injured in these cases meant maimed – armless, legless. She wanted Hugh whole, she didn't want to have to feed and clothe his helplessness for ever. God forgive her, she'd rather him and the boys were dead. You're dead selfish, she told herself.

Dead. The word didn't make sense to her. There were so many ways of saying it – passed away, snuffed it, kicked the bucket. Killed, slain, murdered. These were the real words. She could never forgive or forget. How could they go round planting bombs, that took some people's lives and ruined those of everybody around them? How could it be happening in Derry, where everybody knew each other, where people called to each other from doorways and windows, chatted in queues and shops?

In the seat opposite two boys were playing cards. The smaller one, his brittle tow coloured hair sticking out like wings on either side of his head, turned to his mother.

'He's cheating Mammy, just luk at him.'

The Two O'Clock Train

The older darker boy protested.

'I was not cheatin'. Just because you're not winnin', you think everybody else is cheatin'.'

'Will ye shush,' said their mother, not even looking up from her knitting, 'if youse won't be quiet, I'll take away the cards.'

Anne watched as the needles clicked on a moss green sweater. For Christmas she had knitted Hugh an Aran sweater to wear on the boat. Maybe he would never wear it again. She saw him suddenly in a pool of blood but she could not see where he'd been injured. He wouldn't be able to put the sweater on by himself, she would have to pull it over his square curly head and angle his short tanned arms into the sleeves. Would his hands be able to grip the weather-beaten stump of the tiller as the earth brown sail billowed before them?

The train slid slowly out of the city, past the black shadow of Cavehill, past the dull ranks of housing estates. Away to the right, she could see the gantries of the shipyards, giant yellow gallows against the sky.

It was all her fault. If she hadn't been coming to Belfast, she would have walked the boys to school as usual and Hugh wouldn't be in the hospital, everything would have been fine. She got to the edge of a picture in her mind of how the street outside her house looked now. Then she pulled herself back. Behind her two women compared ailments.

'I told Alice,' said the thin voiced one, ' that me teeth were killing me.'

The other woman wasn't listening.

'Me leg was that sore,' she said,' that I thought I'd have to have it cut off.'

Anne thought of sawn off limbs. Killing me, killing me, have it cut off, have it cut off, the train repeated in rhythm. Her numbness dissolved and anger sparked again. She turned to look at them. Two wizened old women. They'd had their lives, they had children and maybe grandchildren, their whole existence hadn't been torn apart by a bomb. With their yellowing teeth, and creaking bones and down-at-heel shoes, why had they been spared? She wanted to scream out what had happened to her.

Instead she bent down and reached into her shopping bag. Her hand touched the stiff rustling material of the anorak she had bought for Joe. It felt like a shroud. She'd written the cheque to pay for it and handed it to the salesgirl.

'I hope it fits him,' Anne had said, 'because it's a long way back to change it.'

The girl smiled at her.

'You're from Derry,' she said, 'wasn't it terrible about that bomb this morning?'

'What happened?' She got the same sick feeling of panic she always had about bombs – as if a huge lead weight had been lowered into place inside her.

'Did you not hear about it?' the girl said carelessly, ringing up the amount on her till. 'It was a booby-trapped car. A man and his two sons. Isn't it shockin?'

'Oh my God,' Anne had shouted. She'd wanted to lean forward and take her by the throat, a young white throat encased in a frilly cream blouse. The girl's nail-bitten fingers touched the tiny gold heart on a chain round her neck. Her eyes were wide with fright.

'Did they give a name? Did they mention the street?'

'I'm wil' sorry,' the girl whimpered. 'I canny remember.'

Anne only remembered shouting for a telephone and finding herself in the manager's office.

'Is that you?' her sister's voice had whispered, high pitched, 'we didn't know how to find you. We'll come up and get you.'

'Yes. No... Wait a minute.' Derry had never seemed so far away.

'I'll take the two o'clock train,' Anne said, 'I'll catch it if I rush.'

A woman handed her a glass of water. She'd phoned the hospital but nobody there had been able to tell her anything. She knew what the aftermath of car bombs looked like. A film looped through her head, pieces of the wrecked car embedded in walls and gardens yards away, the street spangled with shrapnel. She thought about it in the taxi limping down York Street in a long snarl of traffic.

The train stopped at Antrim. People from the airport came on with tagged luggage and bags from unfamiliar shops. She didn't look at their faces, she didn't want to find happiness in them. When the train moved on again, the boys opposite began to argue and fight. Their mother shouted at them and slapped the older one. She longed to say, do be nice to them, you'll be sorry afterwards. She'd shouted at John this morning because he'd lost his dinner money and at Joe because he hadn't finished his homework. It was the same every morning and then when they walked away into the school yard, she always regretted that she hadn't had more patience with them. What did it matter now?

She could see the head and shoulders of a man down the carriage. He was wearing a cigar brown jacket the exact same colour as his hair. His shirt was a matching beige with a darker brown tie. He looked as if nothing had ever happened to him. All neat and tidy. Not like Hugh. Hugh never looked like that. No matter what she did, his collars always looked misshapen, he lost the buttons off his shirts. This morning she hadn't even kissed him goodbye, she'd been in too much of a hurry for the train and her day in Belfast.

The passing of the train flushed a magpie from a thicket and the old rhyme came into her mind. One for sorrow, two for joy. Such a handsome black and white bird – why should seeing one be such a bad omen? Hugh always laughed at her superstitions, mocked her when she said she'd dreamt of a wedding which meant a funeral, when she swore at the boys for putting their shoes on the table or she forgot and opened her umbrella in the house. Her world was furnished with these small superstitions but she didn't really believe in them. Nothing had warned her about this, she thought, she ought to have had some sign. Life had stopped, not cut off cleanly but with too many unfinished points sticking out like the jagged metal of the car. Would they ever be able to finish painting the boat?

At Coleraine the two old women got out. Children were taking the train down the line after school. John and Joe hadn't even been to school today. She wanted to phone the hospital and say, Please tell me the truth, please tell me how they are. Perhaps the boys were less… damaged than Hugh – he would have taken the brunt of it. Her hands strayed to her purse where she had a photograph of them, but she could see them more clearly in her mind's eye. They both looked so like Hugh. If they grew up, they would look more and more like him, like the young man she'd married.

She left her seat and went to stand in the space at the end of the carriage. The sea came into sight, the mouth of the harbour with a ship riding at anchor, and the sunlight dappling the water. She thumped her fists on the window. She was just a woman going home on the train from Belfast. The sun hadn't stopped shining. Death was so commonplace – people died every day and were buried and in time their belongings were sorted out and dispersed. A year or two later there was no outward sign that they had ever lived except perhaps for a photo on the mantelpiece or the one that lay crumpled in her purse.

As the train went into the tunnel beyond Castlerock, the lights flickered and faded. Anne hoped they would never come on again, hoped that the train would tumble slowly into the bowels of the earth. She wanted to stay in the darkness forever, never to have to see anything that would remind her of Hugh. She could see his face on the tunnel wall, his hair standing up in wiry curls, she could feel his arms round her in his bearlike grip. The roaring of the train gave way to a singing in her ears and then to the sound of the sea as the train came out of the tunnel above the beach.

She pulled down the window and reached for the door handle. The fresh air fanned her face and cooled the pent up tears behind her eyes. The tang of the sea floated up to her. She gripped the handle tightly and pressed it downwards very slowly. With her left hand she caught the edge of the doorframe as the door pulled free of the lock. She could see the cliff face round the curving track. The train hurtled on, the arched hole of the next tunnel coming nearer.

The Two O'Clock Train

Anne could see the sooty brickwork, the sculptured keystone of the arch, the shining rails stretching into infinity. She gripped the door frame and prepared to leap into the darkness when it came.

Hugh's smiling face still watched her from the tunnel wall. He was holding the boys' hands, his hair ruffled, his collar all crooked. The slow black despair lifted and a thought clear as crystal took its place. Hugh might be all right, they might not be dead. Feeling as though she was breaking in two, she drew back from the edge of the abyss. In the tunnel the train's whistle whooped, the cry of an owl. She slammed the door shut.

She stood there for a long time. When she went back to her seat, the cigar brown man glanced at her. The train was crawling now through the fields at the edge of the lough, like a swimmer out of breath on his homeward stretch. The boys opposite were asleep, one on each side of their mother. A late afternoon hush filled the carriage. On the other side of the water she could see the Donegal hills. Over there where they went sailing in the summer, in another country, it was peaceful. She was sure they would go there again. They would put on their bright yellow life jackets and nudge the boat into the water, hoist the earth brown sail.

The lough narrowed to a point where the city rose. The short span of the single bridge locked the two sides together in its iron grip. Seen from the train, Derry still looked like the nineteenth century engraving that hung in her hallway. The filigree spires of the two cathedrals claimed the upper air, the red sandstone bulk of the Guildhall stood foursquare on the quay, the lines of the ancient walls were etched in black. The single tower block of the hospital, where her husband and sons lay, marred the skyline. The city still looked the same as she had left it that morning, every brick in place, each row of houses poised at the same angle, the cemetery still high on the hill on the southern side.

The train crept the last mile. The knot of anguish in her body twisted and tightened. Stepping down into the station was far more difficult than jumping from the train in the tunnel might have been. A tight knit phalanx of loving faces moved forward as she appeared and bore her onward and outward from the station in a melting torrent of tears.

The Horizontal Method

Ma thinks I'm going out with Deukie Doherty.

'When's he taking you out next?' she asks, twirling a length of her greying hair round her finger as if she were trying to turn it into a corkscrew. Deukie Doherty! Dear God in Heaven. It shows that Ma doesn't rate me too high in the stakes for the eligible young men of this town. She is that glad I've got somebody, anybody, she doesn't care if it's Deukie Doherty. I don't even know what his real name is. In my mother's opinion, Deukie Doherty is safe. His father and my uncle are great pals and our grandfathers went to the same school. Deukie has pebble glasses that make his eyes look like specimens in a jar.

'He's taking me to the pictures tomorrow night,' I tell her. He is even safe in the pictures. Ma knows that D. D. is not the kind that wants to sit in the double seats in the back balcony. He couldn't see anything from there, not that you need to. I used to wonder why my sister Eileen, who's married now, always had to get the story of the film from her friend Marge when she sat in the back balcony with a boy. Now I know. How do I know? I'll come to that in a minute.

I met Deukie at a dance that Ma and Da took me to. They do the best they can for me, considering that I am twenty two and broad in the beam and on the shelf. At least I don't wear glasses otherwise my imaginary kisses with Deukie would be like the Clash of the Titans but my hair is as straight as a die and the colour of a dead mouse. My sisters have red curly hair and they are as skinny as rakes and got married as soon as they left school.

'Annie's the clever one in our family,' Ma says. I know what she means. It's not just because I work in a bank. She means that if you have red hair and creamy skin and long eyelashes, you can be as thick as a plank and still get a man. If you look like a Mullingar heifer, beef to the heels, you need to know more than your tables and how to add and subtract.

Anyway Deukie asked me out to dance all of three times and Ma has us coupled in her head forever. Another good thing about him is that he hasn't got a car. Ma thinks so. Fellas with cars, she hints darkly, are bad news. I used to think that she meant that they would drive you into a ditch on the way home from the Derrynane Dance Hall when they had too much drink taken. I would've liked to have asked her why but you don't ask questions like that in our house. You don't ask why my mother switches off the TV right in the middle of a play when the fella and the girl are getting interested in each other. She doesn't want the rest of us to go to hell so we have to suffer along with her.

'There's a good picture on at the Strand this week,' Ma tells me. My heart sinks. Not The Song of Bernadette again? She's seen it at least ten times.

'What's it about?'

'It's all about this... oh I don't want to spoil it for you... this ballet dancer.'

I will have to go and see it with Mary Ann and Bridget so that I can discuss it with Ma. Go over the weepy bits with her. She is a great crier in the cinema, is Ma. She takes one of me Da's handkerchiefs and by the time she's finished with it, it looks as if it's been washed and put through the mangle.

That is how I feel when I've been out with Bernard Connolly. I can hardly say his name out loud, not even to myself. He works in a solicitor's office in Omagh and he has a terrible reputation. He's got it all organised. The Deukie Dohertys of this world don't stand a chance beside the likes of Bernard Connolly. Last week we went to Benalla Head and he brought a picnic, a flask of coffee and a boxful of wee iced cakes. There were even lacy napkins to hold them. We ate the cakes afterwards as if we hadn't seen food for a week. Bernard has a big car with seats that fold down. Another time he brought a bottle of white wine wrapped up in wet newspaper to keep it cool and tiny egg and onion sandwiches. He keeps a thick dark blue and green tartan rug in the back of the car.

    I haven't been to confession since I met him. He came into the bank one day and after I'd sorted out what he wanted, he asked me to go for a drink with him in my lunch hour. I was that surprised, he could have held the bank up then and there and I wouldn't have been able to move a muscle. Luckily Ma doesn't go to the same Mass as me or she'd have noticed that I never go near the altar rails any more to take Communion. But sure what's a wheen of mortal sins compared to doing it with Bernard? No use thinking of hell fire when we're getting the windows in his car all fogged up. The first time we did it I thought, this is what they're all talking about. To tell the truth, I wasn't wild excited about it at the time – it took me a while to get used to it but now I could do it to a band playing.

    Talking about hell fire, I spoke too soon. Ma is doing the Jesuits' retreat for women at All Saints this week. Them Jesuits give them hell every night. She wanted me to go but I told her I had to study for my exams. You're always doing some exam or other for the bank and it's the greatest excuse. Such a wee lie compared to all the big ones I've told her. And who did she see, she tells me this morning, who did she see on her way home but Deukie Doherty and two other fellas walking down the street.

    'So where were you last night?' she says, looking at me very hard. Where indeed? Rolling round on the tartan rug on the far side of Glenarne Golf Course. And me Ma's head filled with all the Jesuits' ranting about going with men – they probably told them they should never touch a man from the neck up, never mind from the neck down. I wonder what do they tell the men? It doesn't seem to

The Horizontal Method

have much effect. Then I come to my senses. What am I going to tell Ma?

'I made a mistake, Ma.'

I'm not looking at her but at the photo of my grandparents' wedding on the mantelpiece. Did they ever get themselves into scrapes like this when they were courting? I doubt it. They look as if butter wouldn't melt in their mouths and a pound wouldn't choke them.

'I thought we were supposed to be meeting outside the GPO. I waited there for ages and then I thought he must have forgotten so I went on to the dance. I met Mary Ann coming down the street and we went in together.'

'You mean that fella stood you up?' cries Ma.

'No, he was waiting for me at... at the hotel. He saw those fellas going into Rooney's and he had a drink with them before going to the dance. He was wil apologetic when I saw him.' The last words come out in a rush.

'You should have et the head off him for keeping you waiting.' Ma is mad, she always takes things to heart. 'Is that fella not a teetotaller?'

'Teetotallers do go into pubs, you know. They're not barred,' I say.

'God, wait till your father hears about this.'

'Hears about what, Ma?' I say. I am tired of talking about something that never happened. My powers of invention sometimes fail me though when I was at the wee nuns' Sister Ignatius said I had the best imagination of anybody in our class when it came to explaining why I didn't have my homework done.

'That that fella stood you up.' Ma's jaw is clenched like a steel trap.

'For God's sake, you'd think he'd committed a crime! It was just a mistake.'

I sigh. I think of one of Ma's sayings. It might have been invented just for me.

Oh what a tangled web we weave

The Horizontal Method

When first we practise to deceive.

'You should tell him to call at the house. I don't like to think of my daughter standing on street corners.' She's pulling her hair into corkscrews again. As if I could ask anybody to call for me at our house, Da would have them in the front room in two ticks, questioning them about their A levels and their prospects.

'Were ye dancing with anybody else?'

If I ever have to be under interrogation it will be a piece of cake compared to Ma and Da.

'Aye, I was dancing with a fella from Portara.' The words come out of my mouth as if somebody else were saying them. God help us, now I'm going to have to invent another fella. The kettle is boiling on the hob so I make us a pot of tea. Ma had her breakfast hours ago, but it's Saturday morning and I'm taking it easy.

'Was he nice looking?' Ma says innocently, reaching for two cups off the dresser. She'll be better when she gets the tea down her. I swear to God, tea is her drug. She drinks about fifty cups a day, worse than me Da's fags.

'He was all right.' I wrinkle my nose. Really I'm thinking about what Bernard and I got up to on the dunes at Craw Bay.

'Did you make it up with Deukie?'

'I never fell out with him in the first place, did I? D'ye think we'd fall out over a wee thing like that?' I'd never fall out with Deukie Doherty unless Bernard Connolly took off for Mars. I know when I'm well off. Everybody in Derrynane has heard about Bernard Connolly and his goings on with women, but I don't care. I'd go through hell and high water for him. I can't understand what he sees in me, but he says he hates thin women.

'If I meet him again, I'll give him a piece of my mind.' Ma pours out the tea and puts in two spoonfuls of sugar.

'Give who a piece of your mind?' I say absently.

'Deukie Doherty! Who else?'

'For God's sake, Ma, he doesn't know ye from Adam. Besides it's my business, not yours!'

I'm really mad. I hate answering her back but I have to stop her from even thinking about talking to Deukie Doherty.

'What did they talk about at the retreat?' I ask, taking a biscuit from the blue tin.

'He was going on about mortal sin. Sins of the flesh.' She eyes me sideways. A subject after my own heart.

'What did he say?' I lay a bet with myself that she won't tell me.

'You sometimes wonder,' Ma says, chewing on a piece of burnt toast left over from breakfast, 'how them priests know what's going on. I mean they're not supposed to have anything to do with women, they're supposed to be as pure as the driven snow.'

I nearly snort out loud. Thank God she's off the subject of Deukie. She can talk about the sermon and the shortcomings of the Jesuits till the cows come home, I'm all ears.

I tell Bernard about it the next time I see him and he laughs.

'She's going to find out soon, sure as eggs is eggs. We'll have to think up a better story.'

Bernard ruffles my hair. We are in his car at Craw Bay, watching the Atlantic rollers crashing on the beach. He opens my blouse and kisses my left breast. He strokes the other one with his hand. I am not complaining. He does it in a slow deliberate way that burns me up and makes me forget completely about Ma and Deukie.

'Tell yer Ma that you're breaking it off with Deukie,' Bernard says on the way home. 'Tell her you have to study for your exams.'

'I told her that already. But I do have to go to the classes.'

'Take more classes,' Bernard says, tooting the horn at a stray donkey, 'take French lessons.'

'French lessons?'

'I'll teach you,' he says, turning to wink at me. 'I have a great new system. Tell your ma.'

Ma can't understand why I broke it off with Deukie. But, dear God, it's lucky I said that I did because two weeks later, wasn't his engagement in the paper. You could have knocked me down with a feather! Getting married to some girl called Melissa McLaughlin. I wonder what in God's name she looks like if she's marrying him. I had to pretend to take it very badly and stay in a few nights.

Now I'm taking French lessons. I'm very keen. Ma feels so sorry for me. I told her I was going to the Technical College three nights a week. I'm worried that Bernard will get tired of me.

'I'm going to France for me holidays next year,' I tell her and I can see her eyes lighting up – I might meet a man. Then I can see her thinking that he would be one of those dead sexy French men, not such a good idea.

She smiles at me. I'm so relieved not to have to make up stories about Deukie Doherty any more. I really hate the poor fella and it's not his fault. And now Ma hates him too. It's still all I can do to keep her from going round to his house and giving him a piece of her mind. She will be scouring the papers every day for months to see if there's a photo of the wedding. The handsomest couple in the town, I've no doubt.

Bernard is giving me French lessons. He's spent a lot of time in France. We're going to Paris for our holidays, he says. I just hope me Ma never finds out. Bernard whispers sweet nothings to me in the car at Craw Bay and Benalla Head and Glenarne Golf Course. Je suis, tu es, il est. I have to get the verbs right beforehand. A bit like Forfeits. The Horizontal Method, he calls it.

Bad Dreams

The bell rang and somebody banged on the door. I'd been dreaming of black jagged cliffs where the sea glittered far below, the same dream I'd dreamt every night for three months so I was glad to wake up. My little brass clock showed half past ten and I'd turned off the alarm hours ago. On the bedside table there was a stack of books with markers in them, old cinema tickets, faintly printed receipts. No exams today. I pulled on a ragged dressing gown over my nightie and went into the hall. The stained glass of the door made a blue and red pattern on the right hand wall. I wanted it to be the postman with an early present for my twenty first birthday on Saturday, but there were two figures out there.

My eyes blinked in the sunlight. My uncle Malachy stood on the doorstep, his crinkly waved hair like an old-fashioned film star's. He wore a suit and his teeth were whiter than a smoker's should have been. Beside him was Charlie Donan who was not even a relative by marriage, maybe a step-cousin. What had happened to bring them here at this time on a Monday morning? My heart was a lead weight.

'Gemma!' Malachy said. 'We've been looking for you.'

I said nothing, willing him to tell me the bad news. They looked at each other, then back at me. Charlie's bald head shone in the June sun, I could see the little white bristles sticking up, like Desperate Dan's chin in the comics.

'Your ma's ill, we've come to take you home.'

I brought them into the kitchen. The curtains in the bed sitting room hadn't been opened for days and the air was stale, the furniture draped with dirty clothes.

'I'll just get ready.'

'Will I make you a wee cup of tea?' Malachy said.

'Tea?' I'd never seen a man make a cup of tea. My father never went near the kitchen. 'That'd be grand.'

I cleaned my teeth, washed my face under the cold tap. I knew there was something terribly wrong but I couldn't ask them. I pulled on dark clothes – a navy serge skirt wrinkled from hanging over a chair, a green T-shirt stained under the arms. I'd take the blue T-shirt too, it was clean. Cover the dirty one with my navy cardigan. Not my sandals, but the black high heels.

I drank a cup of too hot too sweet tea. Malachy, God bless him, had rinsed three cups. I grabbed two slices of white bread, spread two triangles of Dairylea cheese on one, and glued them together. I lifted the sandwich to my mouth, then stopped.

'Excuse me,' I said, before I bolted to the bathroom and retched over the toilet bowl.

In the car I was quiet. After we passed through Toome, I felt hungry enough to eat my sandwich. Charlie and Malachy whispered to each other. We didn't stop at the hospital but drove smoothly past. I relaxed and sank back into my seat. Under my breath I hummed She Moved Through The Fair, even though I sensed that things weren't right, they would never be the same again. The sun wouldn't shine, I would never go back to university, finish my exams, put on the black gown with the pale blue ribbon, or the mortarboard.

We were just turning into Gilfennan Road when Malachy looked at me and said in a low voice, 'It's your mother, Gemma, she's gone. I'm really sorry.'

I sat there crushed. I was hoping that my mother would be at home in her own bed, with the doctor there, even though I'd guessed she was dead. My mother was gone, she would never again be there to tell me off like she used to do, asking why I hadn't done my homework, mended the hole in my gloves, covered my school books in brown paper. Never again would she tell me not to be wearing make up, it upset my father, to eat with my elbows in, hold my knife and fork properly, chew everything thirty two times, not to say aye and naw for yes and no.

The hall was full of people. They shook my hand. 'Sorry for your trouble,' they said, 'it's a real pity about your mother.'

Father Pat came forward.

'Oh Gemma,' he said in his thick Cork accent, 'can I do anything for you?'

I looked at him, but didn't speak. Charlie handed over my bag, touched my shoulder. I didn't know whether to call him Charlie or Mr. Donan, so I just said thank you.

'Gemma,' said Aunt Cassie, her fat face contorted with misery.

'Wee Gemma,' said a distant cousin behind Cassie. I smiled, but I wanted to scream. Cassie led me into the back bedroom. There was a hot smell of candles and white lilies. The curtains were drawn, the mirrors draped with white sheets. I looked down at the small woman in the bed. My mother had shrunk into someone else.

'What?' I said.

'Wheesht, child,' my aunt said.

'What happened?'

Cassie shook her head. 'Not now.'

Father Pat came into the bedroom. He knelt down on the brown threadbare carpet and said a prayer in Latin.

'When did she...?'

Cassie took me by the arm, marched me out of the room. I could hear Father Pat starting a rosary, The Sorrowful Mysteries, voices murmuring in reply.

Downstairs in the front room all the furniture was pushed back along the wall, so that the sofa and matching chairs formed a comfortable line like the back row of the cinema. Cassie pushed me into a chair, a neighbour brought me a cup of tea and a buttered

Bad Dreams

treacle scone. I took a sip of the tea. It was too weak and too sweet. What was it with the sweet tea?

'Come into the kitchen,' Cassie said, ten minutes later. She scooped the cup and saucer out of my hand. 'Your father will want to speak to you.'

A little space opened up in the kitchen. I stood in it. The table and the dresser were laden with plates of sandwiches cut into neat triangles, and two kinds of cake – bright yellow sponge and rich dark fruit – enough to feed an army.

Suddenly my father stood before me, staring as if it were all my fault. His black-beetled eyebrows were blacker than ever and his eyes were red. I hadn't cried yet, not in front of all these people.

'Your mother,' he said. 'Your mother...' I waited for the awful truth. Cassie stood beside him. I watched them both. Why would nobody tell me anything? My aunt's eyes travelled from my face down to my toes and came back to rest on my stomach. Her hands flew to her mouth and she cried, 'Dear Jesus!'

Aunt Kitty turned from the sink. I could see the line of white hair growing out in her parting. There was a sharp intake of breath. She and the other women in the kitchen knew about me, they could see something that I could hardly see myself. There was a mound under the waistband of my navy skirt. I was a rat in a trap. My father stared too, but he had no idea what he was looking at.

'I'm sorry about Ma,' I whispered and Cassie was twisting my arm again.

'Come upstairs with me, girl.'

I took a deep breath and stumbled up the stairs. We didn't go into my bedroom but into the spare room.

'We have to find you something dacent to wear. Black... and loose.'

She looked at me and shook her head.

'How could you, Gemma, how could you? If your mother only knew...'

I realised that there was no way now of ever finding out what my mother would have done or thought and tears sprang to my eyes.

'I haven't got anything black. I didn't know she was… They didn't tell me.'

'For God's sake, stop snivellin'. Aren't you in a big enough mess without snivellin' on me?'

Cassie opened an ancient wardrobe and the smell of mothballs nearly knocked me down. She flicked through the rail of clothes and came out with an enormous ugly black serge suit.

'I'm not wearing that!'

'You're not going to be at your mother's wake in those clothes.'

So I put on the suit. It made me look like a Russian shot putter – the jacket had shoulder pads as thick as a club sandwich. The smell made me gag. The skirt was shapeless, which was what Aunt Cassie wanted. She didn't want anybody else to see my shame.

'Sweet God in Heaven, what do I look like?'

Cassie sniffed.

I picked up my clothes and went to my own room, set my bag on the floor. I threw myself down on the green satin eiderdown, frayed at the seams. I found the corner of it that I used to suck as a child, and cried my heart out. I would never have to tell my mother now. This summer after the exams (would I ever finish them?) I would go to London and get a job and stay there till the baby was born. Nobody could make me come home, not my Da or Cassie or Kitty. But there was still the wake and the funeral to get through. I washed my face in the bathroom. I found a white blouse folded in a drawer and put it on underneath the suit jacket.

I thought about the last time I'd seen my mother. About six weeks ago, she'd come to Belfast for the day to buy an outfit for a wedding in July. I'd met her at the station and we'd trawled the shops together. We'd had lunch in a swanky place downtown that my father would never have set foot in, it was so expensive. My mother had found herself a pale blue dress with draped shoulders and a lace collar. I wanted her to buy a pink hat and gloves but she thought it far too frivolous a colour.

'I couldn't wear pink at my age, it's a colour for young girls like you.' She'd smiled at me and ordered two cups of coffee for us because she knew it was the kind of thing you ordered in a restaurant. Normally she never drank the stuff.

'Pity you're not invited,' she said, 'we could have got you a great new outfit as well.'

I'd kissed her goodbye and put her back on the train at six o'clock. I'd missed a whole day's lectures but I didn't care. Now I'd never kiss her again.

I went downstairs and joined the ebb and flow of people who were drinking tea, sipping whiskey. I mingled with friends of my mother, friends of my father, uncles and aunts, cousins I'd never met before. They talked non-stop about my mother, telling stories about her in another life before I even existed.

'She was a really great wee cutty when she was young,' Aunt Kitty said, 'always smiling and joking.'

Before she married my father, I said under my breath.

The day of the funeral was clear and cool, even though it was June. I felt as if I were staying in a hotel. Strangers kept handing me cups of tea and sandwiches and slices of cake. I hadn't eaten a real meal since I came home. Cassie and Kitty kept a tight eye on me, in case I tried to leave the house or telephone anybody. When it was all over, I promised myself, I would catch the train back to Belfast.

I took my ancient navy blue winter coat off the hanger. I hadn't worn it since school. I brushed the dust off the shoulders. I pulled it on over the black suit. No way was I going to walk about in that yoke. I combed my hair, took a quick peek in the mirror and went downstairs. Father Pat was in the hall, and he nodded to me but not as pleasantly as the day I came home. In the kitchen Cassie and Kitty and other relations were huddled together, drinking more tea.

Cassie gasped when she saw me.

'You're not going like that. You look like a refugee.'

'Or an orphan,' I added.

'Don't say that, you'll upset your da.'

Bad Dreams

'He's hardly spoken to me since I came home.'

'Sure the poor man is distraught.'

'What happened to my mother? Why won't anybody talk about it?'

'She had a heart attack. They found her in the street. They say she was talking to somebody and she just fell down.'

I sobbed a big deep sob.

Cassie shushed me, then she said, 'You'll need a hat.'

I went back upstairs and found a wee hat of my mother's tucked away in the back of a drawer. It was soft black velvet, with a feather in it. I put it on and fixed my hair round it. I could smell bacon frying, doubtless my da's and Father Pat's breakfast.

I couldn't eat anything but I might have a cup of tea. My father was sitting at the kitchen table, cutting up a fried egg. The yolk ran over the plate. He speared up a piece of crispy bacon and dragged it through the yellow mess. He turned round and looked at me. A strange cry, like an animal in pain, came from his lips. I rushed out of the kitchen and shut myself in the downstairs toilet. Retched over the bowl again.

I could never please any of youse, I said to myself, never. The smooth smell of Imperial Leather calmed me as I washed my hands. Hanging from a nail was my mother's best guest towel, pale blue, with pink flowers embroidered on it. My fingertips rubbed against the hard little nubs of stitching. I looked at myself in the dim mirror. I could see that I looked like my mother when she was young, especially with the hat on. No wonder my father had been upset. But I wanted to wear it, to remind me of my mother. It was a link to her, a link to the living person, not the figure in the bed who had now been decanted into a pale varnished coffin. The undertaker, a mean-looking man in a shiny suit, had screwed the lid down so tightly it set my teeth on edge.

Cassie was waiting for me in the passage outside. She was dressed in bottle green and looked like a barrage balloon. She whipped the hat off me and I cried out.

'Go in there and have something to eat and stop making a

holy show of yourself!'

Her fat cheeks wobbled. Sugar cheeks, my mother had called her. During the last few days, Cassie must have eaten more than her fair share of cakes. I wondered if the black suit had belonged to her. I had hoisted up the skirt with a green diamante belt so that it was shorter and less shapeless.

'How could you even think of wearing that hat!'

'If my mother could see me now, she'd turn in her grave,' I said and Cassie slapped me on the cheek. I wouldn't cry again, I told myself, not for her. I imagined myself at the graveside in my tight blue T-shirt and shocking pink trousers. That would go down a storm.

In the dining room I found a curled up sandwich on a plate. Even though I never wanted to see another sandwich, I picked it up and took a bite. It was cheese and onion, which meant my breath would smell when I was greeting people but who cared? After it was all over and I'd finished the exams, I'd be off to England to get a job somewhere. No other plans, no future provision for me and Billy Downey's baby.

Behind the dining room door, I drank down two shot glasses of my father's best Bushmills whiskey. I was dizzy with misery. Nobody had remembered my birthday.

My father threw a clod into the grave. It thudded against the coffin. To me it felt as if he were stoning my mother. Without thinking, I threw another after it. The priest had finished his prayers and folded his stole. People milled round us, shaking our hands. I nodded at everybody. I was roasted in my winter coat, I thought the heat must be radiating out from me in waves. Cassie's hands fastened on my arm, like a beggar pleading for alms. I broke away from her and shouted, 'Leave me alone.' Heads turned. My father gaped at me, and shook his head. Kitty came up on the other side and propelled me towards an Austin Princess.

'I never told her,' I muttered. 'It's not my fault. Youse told her, you must have.'

The air was silent, the birds had stopped singing. My father

Bad Dreams

loomed up beside me, his face haggard. I couldn't tell him. The rest of them knew, but nobody had been brave enough to break the news. I ripped off my coat, losing a button in the process. I threw it down. I wanted to throw it in the grave. Something turned in my stomach like a worm. The baby, my God, the baby.

My father stood there, watching me.

'It's my birthday,' I screamed. I wanted somebody to say it. Happy Birthday, dear Gemma. Many Happy Returns of the Day. Though there were no clouds in the sky, the sun seemed to have disappeared. The mourners were melting away among the tombstones.

It was Charlie and Malachy who took me away. Charlie picked up the coat. Malachy took my arm. Behind his parked Morris, he held me. I leaned into him like a starving child. I cried all down his starched white shirt and his threadbare black tie. When I stopped and stood back, he lit a cigarette and passed it to me. We sat in the car till all the others had gone. Charlie winked at me, and they sang Happy Birthday. Charlie and Malachy whom I scarcely knew.

Half and Half

Mr. Holiskey told Nicky Donnelly that he was damned if he'd listen to reason. They were in Dillon's pub at the time and he was throwing the jars of whiskey and Guinness chasers into him at a stiff rate and buying for anybody that would take the time to listen to him. So plenty of people in Dillon's were prepared to listen.

'Tis the house,' he said, 'tis the house. That Sheehie Hanlon read us the will and you'd never believe it.'

'Did you get the house then?' Nicky asked.

'I did not. Would you just houl' yer wheesht and listen to me?'

Others in the bar wished the same so that they could hear what had happened. The whole town was agog with rumours about the Holiskey will.

'I find it hard to stomach that that Sheehie, who took ten years to pass his exams – I could be a better solicitor myself, given the ghost of a chance – had the audacity to read that document to us, never mind the fact that he was instrumental in drawing up this, this affectation, this scandalous piece of paper that purports to be me father's last will and testament.' Mr. Holiskey stopped there, out of breath, for he wasn't a young man any more. He took a long slow draught of his Guinness. The creamy foam left a pale wisp on his upper lip. Everyone within earshot in Dillon's dark smoky bar was waiting for the next instalment. It was like the day of the Gaelic Football Final in Croke Park when the score was 29 all at full time.

Nicky Donnelly would have asked another question but he felt a dozen pairs of eyes levelled at him in warning.

'It's the way it was put,' Holiskey was saying now, 'it's the way he arranged the thing. Diabolical, I'm telling ye, diabolical. It will never stand up in a court of law, never. I'm sartinsure of that. There are many things on this earth that I'm not sartinsure about, but this is not one of them. If I have to take it to the High Court in Dublin,' and here he waved his hand menacingly, 'or even further afield, we'll get to the bottom of it in time.'

The drinkers held their breath and some wished that Nicky would intervene with a question, short and to the point, so that they could be put out of their misery. But they knew Holiskey was not a man to be hurried. And as long as he was buying, what was the price of patience?

There was a clink of glasses in the silence long enough to say three Hail Marys.

'Ye know what he's only gone and done?' Holiskey began again and the crowd sighed with impatience. 'He's only gone and left half of the house to me and half to that sister of mine. I have names for her but they're not fit to be heard in company.'

'That doesn't sound too bad,' Nicky said.

'Ah, but that's not the holy all of it, not by a long chalk. That sister of mine, that ...' Here Holiskey's rage seized him and he fell into a coughing fit. Nicky handed him the whiskey glass so that he could overcome the tickle in his throat. He went purple in the face and wheezed like an old melodeon before he got his breath back.

'Easy on, man, easy on,' Nicky said, 'you don't want to let them people get the better of you.'

'It's all very well for you to say,' Holiskey was mournful, 'but you don't know the holy all of it.'

The crowd shuffled their feet and whispered in annoyance. If only that wee squirt of a Donnelly would keep his mouth shut and let your man get on with the story.

Half and Half

'The thing is,' Holiskey began, his words slurring into each other like oil and water trying to mix, 'the thing is, who has which half.'

'I can see that,' Nicky said, nodding his head. 'I can see you might have a problem there, right enough. It stands to reason. I mean you might have the top half and her the bottom half and then you'd have a problem. Especially wi' a big house like that. A house that's all one storey or even a wee bungalow, that wouldn't be the same thing at all. Oh aye, any man could see that.'

Holiskey stared at him, transfixed.

'And how did ye know, man, that was what happened?' Holiskey jabbed a finger in Nicky's chest.

'Me? I don't know nothing, nothing at all.' Nicky's voice was fearful.

'A wee bird didn't tell ye? You're sure of that?'

'Honest to God, Mr. Holiskey."

Holiskey wrenched his neck round in his collar and took another drink of whiskey.

'Well now, ye see, isn't that exactly what happened.'

'There could be trouble there, Mr. Holiskey. Whoever has the lower half has the upper hand, so to speak, if you follow me drift.'

'You've hit the nail right on the head,' Holiskey said slowly. 'That damn sister of mine won't let me in the door ever since Sheehie read this stuff out to us.'

'Your own sister now, isn't that a terrible shame?' Nicky said, though he knew that there was no love lost between the two.

'It's more than a shame, it's a diabolical bloody liberty. I'm going to have to get a ladder up to the second floor if I want to get to me bed in future. Can ye imagine a man of my years and stature shut out of his own house?'

'It's a terrible situation, right enough, Mr. Holiskey.'

As Holiskey got more and more belligerent, Nicky Donnelly became more and more respectful. He didn't want to incur the big man's anger, that was plain to see. But the eavesdroppers wished he wouldn't interrupt so often.

'Could ye get a ladder up to the winda?'

'It would have to be a right long ladder to get up to the second floor,' Holiskey said.

'Wait tae we see now, wouldn't Cootie Brennan have a ladder that long? He's always up painting people's gable ends.' Nicky was pleased with himself.

'Is he that fella that lives down in Arthur Street?' Holiskey was doubtful, as if he didn't want to be rescued.

'The very man. I could go and ask him if you like. Sometimes I give him a good tip for the races so he owes me a favour.'

'Och sure he wouldn't lend his ladder to a perfect stranger. I mean it's not as if I just need the lend of it for the afternoon. I'd be coming and going on it all the time, now that would be a botheration. I'd have to be running up and down that ladder every time I wanted a plug of tobacco.'

'Not to mention when you've got ten pints inside you and a few whiskey chasers of an evening,' the barman said in a whisper and the people nearest the counter sniggered.

'Of course, I could take me stuff out,' Holiskey meandered on, 'but I wouldn't give her the satisfaction. There's only one good thing, she canny use the bathroom, it's up on my floor. She'll have to use the outside privy in the yard. That'll freeze her arse off in the winter.' He chuckled and reached for his whiskey glass only to find it was empty so he resorted to the Guinness. 'Put another one in there, there's a good fella,' he said, waving the shot glass around. Nicky carried it to the bar like an obedient dog.

'There's another thing,' Holiskey went on as soon as Nicky came back, 'she's got the kitchen downstairs and the drawing room on the first floor but she's got no bedroom. And I'm not giving her any access. I can just see her stretched out on the dining room table, oh she'll be grand and comfortable there. You could ask yourself just exactly what my father was up to, doing a thing like that.'

The next day the whole town was talking about the Holiskey will and speculating about what would happen. Nicky Donnelly had taken Holiskey home to sleep on his sofa. He'd glared at everybody

Half and Half

when he left Dillon's, telling Nicky that he knew everybody in the town was laughing at him and he would never forgive Sheehie Hanlon for getting him into this situation.

The next thing we heard was that Holiskey had engaged his cousin, Martin Moran the builder, to help him.

'Would you just think about building me a staircase up beside that gable end, Martin,' he was heard saying to him in Dillon's and we all waited for the next development. There was disappointment that he hadn't borrowed Cootie Brennan's ladder to get up and down because the bookie had already taken bets as to how long it would be before Holiskey fell off the ladder and broke a limb, £10 for an arm, £20 for a leg and £25 for anything else. But the sister, Hannah Mary, went into Sheehie Hanlon's office and told him she didn't want anybody putting a ladder on her land nor making holes in the wall without her permission. Holiskey got a letter from Sheehie Hanlon, telling him to stay out of the house, or at least, his sister's part of the house. He was seen to tear up the letter and use it for lighting his pipe. He told Nicky, 'Sheehie Hanlon doesn't know his arse from his elbow. The land belongs to both of us, so she canny keep me off it, isn't it only the house that's divided?'

People laughed when they heard that Cootie Brennan might be putting a ladder up to the second floor and the bookie took more and more bets about the possible outcome. The barman in Dillon's was not allowed to lay a bet on the grounds that he knew how much alcohol Holiskey had in him. Martin Moran sent an estimate care of Nicky Donnelly's house for building the staircase.

These days there was always somebody willing to buy Holiskey a drink and he was rarely sober. He sat on a stool all day in Dillon's until he fell off and some kind soul would give him a hand home to Nicky Donnelly's rickety sofa with its insides sticking out like a dead cow's ribs.

Bunny Tuohy stopped running after him because she said she didn't want to be traipsing up and down a ladder every time she needed a cup of sugar. Mary Anne Bannen said she couldn't understand how any father could do that to his own son. Her sister said, 'Sure he didn't treat his father all that well when he was alive, did he? Do you not remember how the father used to be always sending him out for a wee jorum of whiskey and he would never come home till every bar in Crumnaclaun was shut?'

And all this time no word was heard from the sister. When she went to Mass people left her with the whole row to herself except for Jimmy Coughlan who was off his head anyway. Holiskey himself didn't know if it was night or day. Mrs. Jameson of the Post Office took pity on him one day when he came into to get his pension on a Friday when he should have collected it on a Tuesday. She asked him into her back parlour and gave him a whole feed of bacon and egg and sausage with slices of soda bread and barmbrack washed down with lashings of hot tea.

'It's very good of you, Missus,' Holiskey said, 'and I appreciate it all the more, seeing as my own sister wouldn't even give me the time of day.'

Mrs. Jameson's feelings of generosity melted away like snow off a ditch in spring when Holiskey began to steam in her kitchen. The stench of him, she said later, was just like a common tramp. When he'd thrown all that food into him in no time at all, she told him he should go home and have a bath. Holiskey, always of an uncertain temper, roared at her, 'Woman dear, sure I haven't got a home to go to, never mind a bath. All I've got is a tin bath in Nicky Donnelly's back yard and even that is rusted.'

Mrs. Jameson took it thick and in her turn, wouldn't give him the time of day when he came to collect his pension the week after, even though he was sober enough to come on the right day. The rumour went round that his father had left him all the money even though he only had the top half of the house. Mrs. Jameson sniffed when she heard this and said as far as she knew, all he had was his pension and not a penny extra in his Post Office book and that you couldn't believe all you hear.

Bunny Tuohy told Mary Ann Bannen that maybe she had been a little bit hasty and maybe she was interested in Holiskey after all, wasn't he the fine figure of a man, considering the age of him,

Half and Half

and Mary Anne was to keep her clats off him.

After Mass on Sunday people stood together in tight wee bunches, braced against the cold wind that always blew round the door of the chapel. They clucked their tongues when Holiskey's name was mentioned. In Dillon's fewer people were prepared to stand him a drink and Barney Dillon asked him to pay up for what was on the slate. Nobody knew what would happen next and everybody wondered because there is not a lot to talk about in a town the size of Crumnaclaun.

'The smell of him makes me feel sick to me stomach,' Nicky Donnelly told the barman, 'and me sofa will nivver be the same again.'

'Ach, you've had that oul' thing in the house since your granny got married,' the barman said to him.

Nicky gave him a cross-eyed look.

'Yer woman Bunny Tuohy wants to get the priest to him, to settle him down,' Barney went on, polishing glasses.

'Father Murphy would need to knock their two silly heads together to put some sense into them.' Nicky took refuge in his pint of Guinness.

'It's all her fault,' he added, 'she's keeping Holiskey out of his house and he's keeping me outa mine and God only knows where it will all end.'

'Why don't you go and see her?' the barman said, hanging the glasses above the bar.

'Me?' Nicky looked as if he'd be happier if he'd been asked to rob a bank in broad daylight. 'Go and see Hannah Mary Holiskey? Sure what good would that do? And what would I say to her?'

'She'd be that chuffed that a fella was taking an interest in her at last and you might be able to persuade her to let Holiskey into the house and then you'd have him off your back. Wouldn't he be grateful to you for speaking up on his behalf?'

Nicky scratched his head. He wasn't sure about the wisdom of this.

Half and Half

'Give us another pint,' he said to the barman.

'She's not really such a bad looking cutty, and from all I hear, she's the one that got the money,' the barman went on. 'Georgie Holiskey must have had it stashed away. Do you know, he won the pools once and we never saw a penny of his winnings?'

'The pools?' Nicky said with reverence, 'he won the pools?'

'Nothing to get excited about, only a coupla thousand quid, but as the man said, better than a slap in the face with a wet fish.'

Nicky sipped his Guinness. He wasn't one for moving quickly. It was three days before he got up the courage to call on Hannah Mary.

He stood outside the front door, the door that was barred to Holiskey, too nervous to ring the bell. His hand hovered over it like a restless bird. He'd rehearsed what he was going to say but now he wasn't sure if it was going to work. He'd had a drink in Dillon's on the way up to give him some Dutch courage.

'Just a wee whiskey,' he'd said and Barney had winked and said out of the corner of his mouth, 'Good on ya, Nicky.'

Now he had a hollow where his stomach used to be and he wasn't sure if any words would come out when he tried to speak. He adjusted the handkerchief in the breast pocket of his best suit and rang the bell.

Hannah Mary Holiskey took a long time answering. It seemed to Nicky Donnelly that he'd been standing there for hours. He'd got rid of Holiskey by giving him a good tip for the races at Leopardstown so he knew he'd be watching the television in Larcey's betting shop.

When the door opened, Nicky wished he'd never come. Hannah Mary stood there, all six foot of her. She wasn't quite as wide as she was long but her shoulders were broad enough to carry a coffin. Her grey hair was cut as short as a monk's tonsure and her beady black eyes reminded him of his mother's clocking hen. Nicky couldn't remember whether he had ever spoken to her, apart from her father's wake. She hadn't looked happy then and she didn't look happy now.

Half and Half

'Miss Holiskey,' he said and cleared his throat. His voice was weak and shaky. He tried again. 'I hope I'm not disturbing you. I just wanted to speak to you about something.'

'What about?' She sounded like a dog barking.

Nicky almost turned on his heel to walk away, he was so terrified.

'It's about, it's about your brother.'

'And what makes you think that I might want to hear anything about my brother, tell me that?'

The way she moved her head put Nicky in mind of a fox hunting chickens.

'Well, I…'

'Did he send you?'

'Naw, he knows nothing about it.'

'Come on in then.' Her tone was grudging but she pulled the door back. Nicky noticed that there was a brand new chain on the inside. Hannah Mary was taking no chances. His heart sank and he wished he was back in the snug in Dillon's drinking a hot whiskey.

She led him into the kitchen. He wondered about the arrangement of the rooms above which Holiskey had described but this was hardly the time to ask for a tour of the house.

'Would you take a cup of tea?' Hannah Mary asked.

'I would.' Nicky stood beside the stove, moving from one foot to the other.

'Sit yourself down then. The kettle's nearly boiled.'

When he had drunk a cup of tea, she said to him, 'Now what's all this about that brother of mine?'

Nicky looked all round the room, out of the window and then back at her.

'Well, it's like this, Miss Holiskey, he's sleeping on my sofa at the moment and I was wondering when that would come to an end. It's not that I want to get rid of him, you understand, but it was only a temporary arrangement, just to tide him over, and he's been there for three weeks now…'

'And what is it you're expecting me to do?'

Half and Half

'Maybe you could see your way into letting him back into the house. You could maybe sort things out between the two of youse.'

Hannah Mary threw back her head and laughed.

'He can do whatever he wants to, as far as I'm concerned.'

Nicky couldn't believe his ears.

'You mean...?' he stammered.

'I mean he can come and go when he wants to but he's not coming through my part of the house,' she declared. Nicky felt as if he'd just been run over by a cartwheel.

'Will you tell him that?' she asked, fixing him with that hard stare.

'I will, I will surely,' he said. He could count on one finger the chances he had of remaining in one piece when he told that to Holiskey.

She was seeing him to the door before he got up the courage to ask, 'Are you interested in the cinema at all, Miss Holiskey?'

'It's very rarely I go but I enjoy it when I do.'

'Would you be interested in coming to the pictures with me in Ballybrae on Tuesday next?'

'Well now, you surprise me, Mr. Donnelly. The pictures, is it? Ballybrae on Tuesday? Why not?'

Nicky was astonished at his success.

'I could come and get you in the van...'

'That won't be necessary. I'll be in town anyway and I'll meet you outside the cinema.'

'Would half seven suit you?'

'That'd be grand,' Hannah Mary said and for a moment Nicky Donnelly wasn't sure if she was laughing at him.

'Thanks for the tea.'

He stood on the doorstep after she'd closed the door and wondered at his daring. He wiped his brow. Then he went to Dillon's where the barman stood him a double whiskey when Nicky told him what had happened.

'Didn't I tell you it would work like a charm? Now all you have to do is get your man to fix it up with Martin Moran.'

Half and Half

'I'm not sure how far I can go with this caper, Barney. Going to see her was bad enough and now I have to go to the pictures with her.'

'Och, no problem, Nicky. All you have to do is sit beside her in the dark and pretend she's a beautiful blonde.'

'It's all right for you to talk, it's not you that has tae do it,' Nicky said with bitterness, 'I should never have listened to you in the first place.' He gulped at his whiskey.

'We'll all get somethin' outa this. You'll get in with her, Holiskey'll be grateful to you, and then when he's back in the house and gets paid his inheritance, I'll get paid. Sure I couldn't go round to her front door and ask her to the pictures, me wi' a wife and five weans, now could I?'

'I don't want anybody knowing a word about it.' Nicky jabbed him in the chest with his finger.

'On the head of me mother, God rest her, I won't tell another living soul,' the barman said.

Holiskey was gloomy when Nicky got home.

'Yer horse never even came near the finishing line,' he told Nicky as soon as he walked through the door.

'I'm sorry about that,' Nicky said, pulling off his boots, 'sometimes they win, sometimes they lose.'

'You told me it was a dead cert.' Holiskey's head was turning round in his collar again like a marionette.

'Listen, I've got news for you.'

'What kinda news? It would need to be better than that tip you gave me, it certainly would.'

'I went to see your sister. She says she has no objection to you coming back to the house. Even better than that, she's going to be out of the house next Tuesday night.'

Holiskey blinked in surprise.

'Did she really say that?'

'She did indeed.' Nicky wasn't going to mention the condition she'd laid down nor the fact that there was now a chain on the door.

Holiskey sat back on the sofa and thought about this news.

'If that isn't a turn up for the books. You know what I'll do. I'll get Martin over and he can start building the staircase when her ladyship is off the premises. Could we make sure that she'd be out all day on Tuesday?'

Nicky sighed. He couldn't be seen in the company of Hannah Mary Holiskey in broad daylight.

Holiskey jumped up from the sofa and slapped him on the back.

'Tuesday,' he roared, 'Tuesday! She always goes to see Sissie Riordan then. So we're saved. You're a genius, Nicky, you picked the right day.'

'She did mention she'd be in Ballybrae,' Nicky admitted.

'There ye are then. It'll take no time at all for Martin to get the work done and I could even climb up the ladder. It would be nice to sleep in me own bed again.'

'Nothing I'd like better meself,' Nicky said under his breath. Holiskey didn't notice.

'Oh I've got plans, I've got plans,' he chanted, rubbing his hands. Nicky didn't ask him what the plans were. He just hoped he wasn't included in them.

On Tuesday he went to Ballybrae as scheduled and met Hannah Mary and took her to the pictures. He wasn't obliged to bring her home in the van, she had her own car.

'Thanks for taking me to the pictures,' she said as primly as an eighteen year old.

'You're very welcome,' Nicky said. He was so relieved that nobody was going to see him leaving Hannah Mary home that he would almost have kissed her.

'Maybe we could do it again sometime,' he said. He was amazed at himself.

'Not a bad idea. Till next Tuesday then at the same time,' she said, as nice as ninepence. Nicky could only nod his head as she drove away.

It was all over the town the next day that Martin Moran was building a staircase up the Holiskeys' gable, that Hannah Mary had forbidden him to continue, saying that he was violating her property and he would be receiving a solicitor's letter. Holiskey himself had apparently climbed up the ladder and slept in his own bed.

'You'll never believe what I did,' he told the barman at lunchtime, 'you'll never believe it in a million years.'

The barman looked at him and sniffed.

'Try me,' he said. Holiskey had changed his clothes for the first time in weeks and was wearing a clean shirt. He didn't smell and his hair was slicked across the top of his head.

'I took a bucket of Martin's cement and hauled it up on yon ladder and it was no joke, I can tell you that. And then Martin sent that young fella of his up with a couple of hods fulla bricks and we bricked off the opening at the top of the stairs.'

'You never did!' The barman staggered a couple of steps, as if somebody had hit him over the head with a bottle. He turned round and poured a measure of his best whiskey. Holiskey no doubt thought it was for him, on the house, but the barman drank it down himself.

'I could murder a glass meself,' Holiskey hinted and the barman poured him one.

'Are ye sure now you're telling me the truth?'

'As true as God and his Holy Mother.'

'And what about your sister?'

'She must have come up the stairs last night and got the shock of her life. Oh, I tell you, I had the grand bath last night.'

And Holiskey downed his whiskey in one gulp.

After that we didn't know what to think. Was Holiskey going to sleep in his own bed every night? Was Nicky going to get his sofa back? Then Barney the barman let slip that Nicky was taking Hannah Mary to the pictures every Tuesday night, no matter what was on. People from Crumnaclaun who never went to the films were slinking into the back of the cinema in Ballybrae, so they could catch a glimpse of the couple. But there was nothing to see, because it was dark and when the lights came up they were sitting there looking very prim and proper.

'What would you expect from a Holiskey?' Bunny Tuohy said with a snort when it was mentioned, 'sure we know they are not the friendliest of creatures.'

Mary Anne Bannen was in the Post Office at the same time, buying stamps. She turned to Bunny and said, 'You keep changing your tune, darlin'. What is it, are you not sure where the money's at?'

Bunny drew herself up to her full height of five foot two and said she didn't have to stand there listening to the likes of that rudeness. Holiskey came in for his pension two minutes later and Mrs. Jameson served him without even saying hello, but she noted that Bunny was all over him, asking how his back was from sleeping on the sofa. She was behind the times, because anybody that was interested knew that Holiskey was climbing up the bit of the steps that was finished, and on up a short ladder to get in the landing window to his bed every night.

Two weeks later, on the Tuesday, Holiskey didn't come into the pub at all, and Barney Dillon wondered what had happened to him. He still had a big tab on the slate and was only paying off a tenner every week when he got his pension. In the evening as he was polishing glasses, Barney realised that Nicky was there, and not in the cinema in Ballybrae.

'Is it all over then?' Barney whispered as he served him a pint.

'Is what all over?' Nicky said, all innocent.

'Love's young dream. You and Hannah Mary?' Barney winked at him.

'Would you hould yer wheesht and give me head peace,' Nicky said, most unlike his usual self. He sounded almost as crabbed as Holiskey.

Barney changed tack because he knew that everybody in the bar was all ears.

'Have you seen Mr. Holiskey lately? He hasn't been in for a couple of days.'

Half and Half

Nicky took a swig of his pint.

'Has he not? I don't see much of him, since he got back into his room. Right glad to get rid of him I was to tell you the truth. But now...' He stopped.

Barney leaned over the counter.

'Now what?'

'Nothing, nothing at all.' Nicky laid his head down on the bar.

The whole barful seemed to give an enormous sigh.

On the Sunday a thunderbolt fell on Crumnaclaun. Didn't Nicky and yer woman march into the chapel as bold as brass and sit down together right in middle of the front row. The nerve of them! The sniggers could have been heard in Ballybrae, if not Belcreesh.

Father Murphy started saying Mass and it went quiet. And then he read out the notices after the communion, when we were all champing at the bit to get out and start gossiping about them. He read the banns for their wedding! Miss Hannah Mary Holiskey, spinster of this parish. If anybody knows of any impediment... And the same for Mr. Nicholas Aloysius Donnelly, sure we couldn't even think who that was for a minute or two. Married! The two of them. The crowd outside the chapel took a long time to disperse. The subjects of their ruminations left by the side door and walked along the back road. Nobody followed them except a stray dog.

'Married! Would you credit it?' Mrs. Jameson said, her bosom heaving like a steam engine. 'Her father only lately departed and she's getting married!'

'God help us, has that woman no respect!' Mary Anne Bannen cried. Martin Moran was heard to say that he hoped he would get paid for his work before any of these shenanigans took place. He complained that he hadn't got his ladder back either. Nicky wouldn't speak to nobody. There was a notice up in the Post Office to say that his oul van was for sale at a very reasonable price. And on Tuesday morning when the rubbish lorry came round, wasn't his oul granny's sofa dumped outside his front door like a dead animal.

Half and Half

When Nicky Donnelly slunk into the pub two days later, Barney was by his elbow to serve him in two seconds.

'How are you doing, son? That was a bit of a surprise, in the chapel. The usual, is it?'

'It was a surprise to me as well. She proposed to me only last week. I was that surprised I said yes. And now I'm wondering if I'm in my right mind.'

'Will her brother be giving her away?'

'Sure we don't know where he is, wasn't he seen getting on a train in Belcreesh. Hannah Mary will find somebody, don't you worry.' Nicky had the look of a condemned man.

Barney was sworn to secrecy about the big day and five minutes later the whole of Crumnaclaun knew and was preparing to put on their best clothes to go to the wedding even if they weren't invited. There was no sign of Holiskey. On the day itself, it was pouring down rain like there was no tomorrow. A grey elf of a man, wearing a suit the colour of turf, an uncle, it was said, of the bride, took Hannah Mary up the aisle. No white frills and furbelows for her. She was wearing her best suit, a dark green Donegal tweed that made her look more like a navvy than ever. Mrs. Jameson said it put her in mind of a well upholstered sofa.

Nicky stood at the altar fidgeting like he had St. Vitus's dance, and Barney was his best man, because he knew all his secrets. They were going to Bundoran for their honeymoon, because the uncle had a hotel there and they could stay for free. Not big spenders, the Holiskeys, always the cheapjacks.

Mrs. Jameson told Bunny Tuohy that Holiskey's pension was building up in the Post Office but she was sure he'd be back to collect it.

'I just hope he's not sleeping under a hedge somewhere and comes back smelling like he did before.'

'A hedge?' Bunny said, her painted-on eyebrows rising into her hairline. 'Do you think something's happened to him?'

'Naw,' Mrs. Jameson said, handing over her stamps, 'he's away sponging off some other poor crittur for a change.'

Half and Half

They came back off their honeymoon after eight days, on the Monday. Hannah Mary's car was spotted going down the Main Street. No sign of Nicky in the pub.

'He's probly not allowed out the door now,' Barney said to the regulars, rolling his eyes. They laughed and went on drinking.

The following Friday Bunny Tuohy told the priest that Holiskey was missing. He called the guards in Ballybrae and the next thing somebody was knocking at Hannah Mary's front door.

'My brother?' she was reported to have said. 'I haven't seen hilt nor hair of him for weeks.'

'Does he not live here then?' the guard, a useless young fella from Kilbarr, asked her.

'He lives upstairs,' Hannah Mary snapped, 'I don't have contact with him.'

'Your own brother?' The guard was astonished.

Hannah Mary looked straight through him and banged the door in his face. The young fella stood there, looking up and down the road. Father Murphy's car skidded to a halt in front of the house. From the other side of the road the half of Crumnaclaun was watching. The priest got out of the car and took the guard round the side of the house, pointed out the makeshift staircase and the ladder to him.

'You're not expectin' me to climb up yon constraption, are ye?'

'I'm too oul for it,' Father Murphy said. 'The man hasn't been seen for ages. We're worried about him. That's the only means of access.'

The fella scratched his head.

'And if he's in there, how would we get him out?'

'Good question,' the priest said, giving us a wee wave. We were all killing ourselves laughing.

The fella removed his peaked cap and gave it to Father Murphy to hold for him. He started climbing up. He opened the window at the top of the ladder with no bother, and disappeared inside. It was well seen that he didn't have an undetermined number of pints and chasers to contend with. It was cold standing in the road but we wouldn't have missed it for all the tea in China.

He came to the window and shouted.

'I think he's gone, your man is gone.'

'Gone,' Father Murphy repeated from his ringside view beside the gable. There were gasps from the onlookers.

The guard glanced down at the waiting crowd and said, 'He's as cold as charity. I'd say he's been dead a good long time.' We thought he was a mite pale. Not used to finding somebody dead – not just dead but practically a skeleton.

'So we don't need to call an ambulance,' the priest said. 'I'll just call his sister.'

'I'm coming down. Going to radio for backup,' the fella said as if he were starring in some TV movie. Mary Anne Bannen sucked her teeth.

'Who does he think he is?' she said under her breath.

Nicky put his hand up as if he were answering a question in class.

'Do you want me to go up?' he asked when the fella swivelled his eyes to rest on him. 'I'm a friend of his…'

'Not at all,' the guard shouted. 'You see, it might be a crime scene. You nivver know, somebody might have murdered him.'

All hell broke loose on the other side of the road. There were imprecations and swear words all mixed up together. It was like watching our very own soap opera. Somebody whispered, 'It must have been that sister of his, I can guarantee you!'

It was a rollercoaster from then on. There were post mortems, after the real one that said he'd been dead too long for them to know the cause, in the pub every night. Barney said he could afford to go to Miami for his holidays, the takings were up so much. Hannah Mary was taken out of the house and pushed into a police car. They said she had a hood over her head, but what would have been the point of that, we would have known by the heft of her who it was. She didn't come home for ages, while they were investigating.

The chapel was full for the funeral, people came from up and down the country. There was photographers in the cemetery. No wake was held, Nicky said it wasn't up to him. There was nothing afterwards either, not even the chance of a good drink unless you paid for it yourself. The meanness of it! It was as if the Holiskeys had planned everything.

Nicky went back to his own house, but it is said by Barney and some of the shopkeepers in the town that he's being very generous with a chequebook with his name and Hannah Mary's name on it. We're still waiting to hear if Hannah Mary will be charged with murder, but the police got Martin Moran to remove the brick wall Holiskey built at the top of the stairs. The bookie is taking bets of all kinds, he's the one making a fortune now, and the bar is very quiet these days. Boring in our town again.